MW01518780

by Deja Elise

Cover design by BrandorasBox.com

This book is a work of fiction. Names, characters,
places and incidents are either manifestations of the
author's imagination and daydreams or are used
fictitiously. Any resemblance to actual persons, living
or dead, events, or locales is entirely coincidental.

Don't Miss A Thing

Keep up with this busy brain of mine. Sign up for access to some
exclusive gems and giveaways at
www.lickherature.com

Other Works By Deja

ONE

Bri's waist length braids swayed left to right as she strutted through the airport in a white faux fur coat, jeans and high heeled knee length boots.

She made it through check-in just in time. It took several tries that morning just to get out of bed. She showered and packed quickly, throwing in a makeup bag, several bathing suits, sandals and a couple of slinky sundresses into a suitcase. She was sure there were several other things she should be packing, but if she thought too long about it, she'd change her mind altogether.

On approach to Gate G, she adjusted her shades and scanned the sea of faces for her friends. Charisse saw her first.

"Yes," she said, popping up from her chair. "Bri made it y'all."

Sunny and Kayla turned in their seats to see her strolling towards them. Their faces lit up something like kids at Christmas. They all got up from their seats and all three of them danced and twerked to a *'Bri is here'* song they made up on the spot. They didn't give two rats about their fellow travelers watching them with either confusion or contempt for their antics. It was vacation time, and the whole gang was here.

Since the first day of law school when they sat in orientation together, they created a bond that would transcend personal relationships, career changes, financial issues and major life shifts.

Upon graduation, their lives took different paths. Charisse and Bri started their own solo law firms. Kayla stopped practicing after she got married and had her first baby. She was now consulting on the side while Sunny went into academia after burning out from the 'big law' grind.

No matter what direction life took them, they always found the time to reconnect and their favorite way to do that was to plan their annual girls trips.

Last year, they decided they'd escape the coming long Chicago winter. They wanted some place warm, with lots of clubs, good food and a beach they could walk around showing their round black asses on. Miami ticked off all those boxes, even though they had already visited several times.

Bri greeted them with big hugs. Kayla held onto her the longest, and it made her want to start crying all over again.

She managed to avoid them for the last month. There was some embarrassment on her part.

They would never say it to her face, but she knew there would always be an 'I told you so' hanging in the air between them when it came to her relationship with Quinton.

They all warned her, suggested she manage her expectations or cut her losses early on when it was clear they weren't on the same page about life. She didn't think she could change him. That would have been a big mistake, but she hoped he'd see how much of an asset she was.

Even before she secured the ring, they were considered the power couple. They looked good together, and were making big moves in their careers. They had the support of family and friends and if that wasn't enough, the sex was fire. If he wasn't the one, what hope was there to find another?

She had barely cracked thirty, but she was exhausted. Waiting on someone to make a decision that could change your life had that effect. At the very least, she was all cried out about it. A change of pace was exactly what she needed.

"Glad you made it. A Miami trip wouldn't be the same without you," Sunny said.

"Aw. You guys know how to make a girl feel loved."

"Gate G, Delta flight departing from Chicago to Miami, now boarding," the woman at the desk announced.

They boarded the plane to find their respective seats. Since they all bought their tickets separately, none of them had seats together. Charisse managed to talk the woman sitting next to Bri to switch seats with her. She didn't want to, but Charisse was relentless. It's what made her so good as a divorce attorney.

As Bri worked at getting comfortable in her seat, her phone buzzed with a text message from her ex.

I miss you. Please call me.

She dismissed it, put it on airplane mode and shoved it in her purse. If she could, she would erase him from her mind. It would cure the constant hurt she tried to bury at the bottom of client work and bottles of Pinot Noirs.

She pulled out her laptop from her carry-on and went to work.

"What happened to a work-free vacation?" Charisse asked. "Don't let Kayla catch you with that thing."

"I just need to finish this up. I'll be done by the time we land."

Charisse scoffed, rolled her eyes. "Sure you will."

TWO

If the Uber ride was any indication for what the week would be like, Bri wasn't sure she'd be able to hang. The coats were already off and pedicures were now exposed in expensive flip flops.

The driver blasted Reggaeton while the girls danced in their seats. No alcohol had yet been consumed and they were already on ten.

She couldn't fault them. They worked hard, so they played harder. When the gray pant suits came off, the freak 'em dresses slipped on and as they loved to say, *'Can't nobody tell me nothin'!'*

The sun in Miami just seemed to blaze brighter than back home. From the window, she stared up at the tall, swaying palm trees whizzing by. It was instantly calming to her weary soul and she couldn't wait to sunbathe like a white girl in the sun.

The driver pulled into a street rowed with condos and drove slowly onto a curved ramp. They got to see where they'd be staying, an all white, twenty something-foot building with a waterfall at the entrance.

"This is gonna be lit ladies," Sunny sang.

The owner of the apartment they'd be taking over for the week met them at the entrance. He looked like a young Antonio Banderes and Charisse couldn't help flirting with him. She was happily married, but she had a thing for latin men who in turn, noticed her. *'I'm married, not dead,'* she'd often say.

His accent was so thick they could hardly decipher the words coming out of his mouth. The most important thing to know was they were free to use the small bar near the kitchen.

The apartment itself was well designed with ultra modern furniture and boasting panoramic views of the Atlantic sea. She made her way to the balcony to take in the vastness of the turquoise waters lapping up at the sandy shores. Small boats sped by cutting through the water.

After a quick tour of the amenities, they received their key cards and settled in for the evening. Sunny mixed some drinks and they spent most of the afternoon catching up on the details of their lives, all of the stuff they couldn't show through curated Instagram or Facebook posts.

Bri talked about everything except Q, and she appreciated the fact that they didn't steer the conversation anywhere near him. By seven, they were ready for dinner and if in the mood, thought they might hit a club.

"Alright ladies," Kayla said, as she straightened her curls with a flat iron. "We're going to go eat at the Yardbird. I hear the food there is uh-mazing and then we'll head down to LIV."

"Yeah, I'm not gonna go," Bri said, sipping on her drink. "I didn't bring anything but a bunch of bathing suits. I think I even forgot to pack my draws. I'm gonna find a Target, get some essentials, come back here, finish up some work, and get some sleep."

Charisse rolled her eyes. "You could've done that at home."

"You're right. I shouldn't have come."

"That's not what she meant," Kayla said.

"I know. I'm just...it's been hard."

"Do you want to talk about it?"

Bri picked at the strings on the pillow she was hugging. "I'm not trying to kill the mood." She took another sip of her drink. "I gave that man three years of my life. Three whole damn years. Three of my best damn years."

"I wouldn't say that," Charisse mumbled.

"How long was I supposed to wait for him to get his shit together? I want kids. My eggs are scrambling over here."

"Bri, you're thirty. You've got some time babe."

"That's what Angie thought. And she's still out here at thirty-nine, single, thirsty as hell and childless."

Charisse laughed.

"Girl, you are not Angie," Kayla said. "You won't ever be Angie. That chick has other issues."

"Well maybe I'm the one with the issues. He wants to be with me, but doesn't want to marry me? Why am I not worthy enough to be Mrs. Taylor?" She suppressed the tears from falling, but the weight and pressure overwhelmed her. "I hate that he does this to me," she said in between sobs.

They all stopped what they were doing, corralling around her as if they knew the drill.

"You are worthy," Charisse said. "If anything, I know that man loves you. Whatever his reasons for stringing things along is not on you. It's on him."

Charisse was right. It wasn't on her, but it didn't change how she felt about it.

"So you think it's completely over between you two?" Kayla asked. "I just can't see you not being together."

"Well, I gave him back the ring."

"We noticed," Sunny said.

"And I told him he could go fuck himself."

"Wow. Okay."

"...And I told him, I think his mom can't cook."

"Aw damn," Kayla said, on the verge of a laugh.

"...And that his dick is crooked."

Charisse shrieked. "No you didn't tell that man his dick is crooked!"

"Well, yeah. You know when it's that big, it starts to curve at a certain point."

They laughed so hard, it made her laugh too. And she kept laughing, falling back against the couch.

The last thing she wanted was to turn this trip into a Q crying-fest. She wiped her face and exhaled.

"Well listen," Charisse said, wiping away laughing tears. "You're gorgeous, you're smart and successful in your own right. Whenever you're ready to get out there, I've got a couple of friends that would love to meet you."

She propped herself back up. "Thanks. But, I'm cool on anything with a penis for the moment."

"Are you sure you don't want to come? I can lend you something. You made it all this way to stay in here?"

"Do you guys not see this view? Honestly, I don't have the energy. I just need to chill for tonight. Mix myself something else strong and dirty, sit out there on the balcony and clear my mind. Y'all go have fun."

"Then we'll just stay," Kayla decided.

"No. Go. So I can use my vibrator in peace."

"Aw hell naw. Ya nasty," Charisse said from across the room.

She wasn't really going to. Regretfully, she forgot to pack it, but it did the trick. They got ready in their tightest dresses and highest heels.

After pleading a few more times for her to come along, they shuffled out of the apartment already buzzing from their pre-partying.

Once they were gone, so was the energy and the joy. She distracted herself by watching something on Netflix from the large screen in the living room, then spent some time catching up on work. When she grew bored of that, she got dressed and Ubered to the nearest Target.

As always, she came back with more than she needed. Along with a toothbrush, sleepwear and underwear, she grabbed a hat, bought a pair of sunshine yellow espadrilles, plastic cups and two bottles of Yellowtail.

Feeling drained and sorry for herself, she decided to call it a night. She washed up and changed into her new pj's. Placing her phone on the side table,

she slipped into bed burying herself under the plush
duvet and closed her eyes.

THREE

It was only eleven when her eyes popped open. She expected to be out for the entire night. After ten minutes of trying to doze off again, she gave up and rolled out of bed. She used the bathroom then made her way to the kitchen to find something to drink.

There was still some of the stuff Sunni mixed sitting at the bar. She poured all of it into a clear plastic cup and made her way out to the balcony. She leaned on the glass rail and took in the panoramic view of the ocean. The water seemed to glitter where the moon light hit it. Off to the right was the Infinity Pool the owner boasted about on the AirBnB page for the place. It seemed relatively free save for one person who was making good use of it.

The view was beautiful, but five minutes in and she was already bored to pieces.

Slipping into a two piece and netted coverup that left little to the imagination, she made her way down with her drink in hand. The elevator let her off at the third floor where the pool was located. Using the key card, she let herself out.

The night air stuck to her skin so the idea of dipping her feet in the pool seemed perfect. The pool was larger than she thought. There was still one other person swimming in it on their way back from the shallow end.

She took in the posh setting. It was well lit with white lights set on black poles surrounding the perimeter. On the far end were large white tents with cush lounge chairs and beds. Just beyond that was the ocean, truly a scene of serenity set in an urban paradise.

Sliding a foot out of her Prada slippers, she dipped a couple of toes into the water. It was on the cool side, but very welcoming. She put both feet in and sat at the edge.

The swimmer ripped through the water like a pro, and swam up to the end where she finally popped out of the water to catch her breath. She shook water from her locs and made brief eye contact before sinking back in for another lap.

She watched her as she made it to the other side and after a short break, made it back. This time she hopped out of the water and sat not too far from her. She checked the time on her watch and sat there for a moment breathing heavily. They acknowledged each other again, and this time, the swimmer smiled in her direction.

She felt compelled to say something, she always did whenever she was alone with a stranger. It was less awkward - less awkward than pretending each other didn't exist at least.

"Where'd you learn how to swim like that? Doing back strokes and breath strokes and all that fancy swimming stuff."

She laughed, showing off a pair of deep dimples. She was pretty, even for a woman who looked like she went out of her way to downplay her beauty.

"I used to be a part of the swim team in high school. I don't swim as much, but for now, it's keeping me in shape while my knee heels."

"How'd you get hurt?"

"At work. I play professional basketball."

"Oh yeah? You play for the WNBA or something?" Bri teased.

"Yes actually. Forward for the L.A. Sharks."

Bri sized her up, taking note of her incredible physique. "Well you look like it."

"I'm not sure if that's a compliment."

"It is. Those arms and abs don't come from sitting at an office desk all day."

looked down at herself as if she hadn't considered the state of her physical condition. "My job does require that I keep it tight."

"Well that's a perk if you ask me. It takes an hour at the gym, three days a week to keep this ass in check. My boyfriend-" She paused for a moment catching herself. "I mean, my ex would complain the minute I lost just five pounds. He'd just look at my ass and say, *'You lost weight?'*

"I like a nice, round, juicy booty myself," she gestured with her hands, "so I can relate."

"I bet you do?" Bri said, with a light chuckle.

She moved her legs through the water. She loved the weight of it as it cleared around her calves and filtered through her toes.

"I've never seen you here before. Just moved in?"

"No, actually. I'm here on vacation. Rented an apartment here for the week with my girls. You?"

"I live here when I'm not playing. I bought a condo on the fifteenth floor last year. Cheaper than trying to buy a place out in L.A."

"Are you from L.A. originally?"

"I am, but my people are from New Orleans. I'll be here though, until I can get back to work. If I get back to work."

"How long will that be?"

"I won't be ready for preseason. No way around that."

"I don't follow sports, but even I know that sucks."

"Yeah. Got injured playing overseas. Got a lot of people either mad or disappointed in me. I have some regrets."

Her mood seemed to shift, her smile gone with her reality. She got to her feet and made her way to one of the nearby lounge chairs. Bri noticed a slight limp to her step as she did. She also found herself admiring the tone of her thighs. There wasn't an ounce of fat on that body.

She picked up a towel and began drying herself. Bri turned her attention toward the dark sky. There wasn't a cloud in sight and even with all the lights surrounding them, the stars could be seen.

"Where are your girls?"

Bri turned to see she had returned to her spot.

"Oh, they went out without me. I wasn't in the mood. I almost didn't come at all."

"What made you change your mind?"

"I don't know. I didn't want to be alone anymore I guess."

"I feel you. After my injury, I spent a month locked up in my apartment. Jesus couldn't get me to leave my bed."

"Sounds like depression."

"That's what everybody keeps saying. But I was just sad. Why can't somebody just be sad without being diagnosed with a mental illness anymore? If there's a reason to be sad, it should be okay to just feel sad right?"

Bri thought about it for a beat. It had only been over a month since the break up, but from day one, everyone's advice was to get over it. A small part of her felt pathetic about even mourning the loss of her fiancé. After all, she was the one who ended it. She was supposed to cry it out, but not too long. As a strong black woman, she had to keep on and carry on.

"I guess you're right. It's not possible to be happy all the damn time."

"Exactly. Life is about contrast. When I'm low, I'm okay with being low so when those highs come around, because they do, then they feel that much better."

"Well damn. That's low key deep."

"Yeah? Maybe when this basketball thing falls through, I can be a motivational speaker."

It was supposed to be a joke, but the solemn timber of her confident voice spoke volumes, that she expected a career change was on the horizon. She was swimming in the very sadness she just preached about and for Bri, it was uncomfortable. She simply didn't know what to say.

Turns out sadness wasn't the problem. Other people's sadness was. She wanted to fill the space with words, lift the mood back up. Her company was a welcomed distraction and she yearned to feel something else other than heartache.

"I'm Abrianna by the way," she said. "My friends call me Bri."

She moved over to be within arms reach. They shook hands. Hers was soft and a little wrinkly from the water.

"That's pretty. I'm DeeDee. Short for Dorothy Divine."

Bri laughed before she could stop herself. "I'm sorry. Are you serious?"

"No, I'm just kidding. Could you imagine me looking like this with a name like Dorothy Divine?" Bri laughed until she got it all out of her system.

"That's a cute laugh...the way you snort a little at the end."

Bri settled down. She hated her laugh, but automatically liked anyone who liked it. "Thank you," she said, swirling the water with her feet.

"You plan on ever getting in?" DeeDee asked.

"Look, I know you can swim, but you know most black girls don't. It is on my bucket list to learn though. Swimming and learning how to ride a bike."

"Wait. You can't ride a bike?"

"No, I cannot. And don't tease me about it. I can't rollerskate either."

"Damn. What happened to your childhood?"

"I was always in my room reading books like a good girl should."

"Pfft. Good girls are just closet bad girls."

"Oh yeah?"

"Absolutely." She flashed another dimpled smile and Bri felt her face grow warm. "What else you got on that bucket list?" DeeDee asked.

"I was supposed to cross marriage off my list as well, but that didn't happen, but I'm not gonna talk about that anymore," she promised herself. "Last year I crossed off Brazil, swimming with sharks and trying snake. It really does taste like chicken by the way."

"I've tried alligator. Tastes just like chicken too."

"All those delicacies always end up tasting like chicken don't they?"

"Yeah, well...not everything."

Bri shook her head. "I'm assuming we're no longer talking about food?"

DeeDee simply laughed.

"I'm gonna have to watch out for you."

There was no denying it, this woman was flirting with her and she didn't mind it in the least. There were a few times in the past when she openly flirted with a person of the same sex.

There was that one time at the club while in college. She looked across the dark, smoky room, and there this woman was, grown and sophisticated, watching her dance with her girls. She was unsure at first, what her intentions were. Did she have a staring problem or was she in fact, waiting for an opportunity to shoot her shot. She got her answer when she turned to find her just a step away, up close and personal, asking her if she'd like to dance. She spent the night playing hard to get, knowing she never planned on being gotten.

Then there was Professor Bea, her Contract Law professor. That woman had all the barely legal women in the class questioning themselves in her designer power suits. They spent all semester catching each others' eyes. They had several staring contests and she lost every one. When she received a grade she didn't like, she was more than happy to march into her office to complain about it. It would never be anything more than that. If that woman ever got up the nerve to ask her out, the answer would have been a solid, no. 'Sorry boo. I'm straight as an arrow.'

She liked the attention though. It was different from the kind she experienced from men daily. Charisse told her this fondness for female attention meant she was probably bi-curious, but she dismissed it.

"Just because I like the occasional occurrence of female attention doesn't automatically make me thirsty for twat," she said.

She liked to flirt. Flirting was fun and innocent, but it was also a slippery slope, one she had no desire to avoid at this point, not when everything she wanted was slipping through her fingers faster than she could hold on to it.

She kicked the water up with her feet.

"You know what helps with getting over things?" DeeDee asked.

"What?"

"Trying new things."

Bri pulled back and looked her over. She was bold, maybe a little too presumptuous.

"What? I'm talking about learning how to swim."

"Oh. Right."

"What'd you think I was talking about?"

DeeDee knew damn well the answer to that. You couldn't see it, but Bri was burning red.

"No, but really. It would be one more thing you can cross off your bucket list."

"When? Like right now?"

"No. Next week. Of course right now. You're here. May as well just do it."

"Yeah, but no," Bri said, shaking her head. "Not gonna happen. I'm going to look ridiculous."

"What's wrong with looking ridiculous? You can't take yourself too seriously. Being too serious about life is what's ridiculous."

"You're probably right, but I'm not getting in that water."

DeeDee looked up toward the end of the pool. "I'm gonna get you in this water." She unwrapped herself from the towel, propped herself up off the concrete and dropped herself into the pool. She sank deep and popped back up. She flipped over and swam under like a fish before emerging again. "Come," she said, with that adorable smile.

"Not gonna do it."

DeeDee swam up to her, right up to her legs and waded there. "How about if I just show you how to float then? It's really relaxing and it's a start."

Bri thought about it for a beat. She's only known this woman for a hot second and she was asking her to trust her with her life. Even more perplexing was the fact that she was seriously considering it.

"The last time I got talked into doing something I didn't want to do, I was twenty-two and drunk out of my mind."

DeeDee swam up closer. "I've got you. I promise."

Bri chewed on her bottom lip and peered at her through slitted eyes.

"Do those dimples always work to get your way?"

"I dunno. You tell me."

She watched DeeDee floating in the water before her.

"If you let me think I'm drowning, but one time-"

"You won't. I promise. I got you. Just jump."

Bri closed her eyes and her heart leapt within the confines of her chest as she began to countdown from ten. By the time she got to five, she changed her mind.

"You know what it is? I'm actually scared of large bodies of water in general."

"No more stalling. No more thinking about it. Just jump."

Bri closed her eyes, pinched her nose and jumped on command. She sank quickly. Before she could flap her arms in fear, she could feel DeeDee's hand at her waist, helping her up to the surface.

She took in oxygen and wiped the water from her eyes. Her heart was in her throat and her legs moved wildly as she searched for something to land it on. She may as well have been floating in the air.

As soon as she got close enough, she wrapped her arms around DeeDee. "Don't let me go," she gasped.

DeeDee held on to her.

"Relax. I got you. You can hold onto me, but just...loosen up your grip so you don't choke me out."

"Okay, okay. Better?"

"Much better. Look at me."

Bri managed to get a hold of herself and focus on her face. Up this close, she could see just how brown her eyes were when the light hit it just right.

"So I'm gonna move with you a little. Don't worry, you can hold on to me. Okay?"

"Okay. Okay. Okay."

"Alright. We're moving."

DeeDee moved through the water with her in tow. "Do me a favor will you? Kick your legs so we can move a little faster."

Bri did so only out of fear. Water splashed behind her like crazy as DeeDee guided her through the water. She brought her to the center of the pool and they waded there for a quiet beat. Bri wasn't scared anymore, but she was shivering and her heart still hadn't returned to it's normal state. She was a bundle of nerves for other reasons.

"This is fun right?"

"Yeah, fun like going to a dentist."

DeeDee laughed. "Do you want to learn how to float on your back?"

"Will I have to let go?"

"Well yeah."

"Then I'm good right here."

They hung out in the pool for quite some time, her arms wrapped around her, holding on for dear life. DeeDee eventually brought her to the shallow end and they hung out on the steps. Bri appreciated how easy she was to talk to and was pleasantly surprised to know that she was familiar with some of her favorite books. This woman had strong ideas and opinions about life, but she was also open to other perspectives and ideas, a quality she admired in those who possessed it.

Once their skin started to wrinkle and she couldn't stop trembling, they called it a night. She held onto her arms wishing she had taken the towel

DeeDee offered her twice before they entered the building. As they waited for the elevator an older gentleman joined them. He acknowledged them with a nod and busied himself on his phone.

They took the elevator up together. She stood in the back corner on the opposite side of DeeDee who hadn't taken her eyes off of her. She didn't shy away from her gaze, nor fight the pull of her attraction toward her. That feeling was there, the kind you get when you've met someone you know likes you and you like back. Kismet. And it was running through her despite her futile attempts to chalk it up as just another one of her cute little lady crushes.

The man got off on the ninth floor. When the doors closed again, DeeDee shot her a devious smile. "Alone at last," she said, like a bad over-the-top soap actress.

Bri was in stitches. Was she really that funny or was she just suffering from a flirting fit of giggles.

The elevator number crept up to fifteen and the doors slid open.

"This is my stop." DeeDee stepped off and turned around to face her. She took a long pause. She had something she wanted to say, maybe. Her eyes fixed themselves on her lips and Bri's insides lurched just to see it.

"It was really nice to meet you."

Bri swallowed hard. "Likewise," she said, as her heart skipped the next few essential beats.

FOUR

Bri entered the apartment to find all the lights on. At the sound of the door closing, Charisse came out of her bedroom.

"Aubrianna Rae Davis. Where have you been?"

"Oh my god. You sound just like my mother."

Kayla and Sunny followed after, already in their pajamas.

"Did I wake you?"

"Nevermind that," Charisse snapped. "We've been worried sick. We tried calling you, but you left your phone up here."

"I know. I didn't want to bring it down and accidentally drop it in the pool. I always drop my phone around pools."

"Wait. You mean to tell me that you've been down at the pool all this time?"

"Well, yeah."

"By yourself?"

"I was talking to someone. What are you guys doing back so early? It's barely one o'clock."

"Kayla left her clutch in the Uber. We had to wait till the driver came back and by the time he did, we were over it."

Bri made her way into the kitchen. "Did you guys have fun at dinner at least?"

"The food was exceptional," Charisse said, "so that was a win. But back to you. Who was it you hung out with all night?"

"I met her down at the pool. She was swimming and we started talking. And we kept on talking."

"Oh I see," Kayla said with a yawn. "You'd rather hang out with a stranger than hang out with us."

"You know that's not the case. We have to go over there later by the way. They have these really nice outdoor beds like they have at Nikki's Beach."

"I'm tired," Kayla said, scratching her scalp underneath her bonnett. "I'm going to bed. Glad you're still alive."

"Good night," Bri said, as her stomach growled. She had forgotten to eat. She looked in the fridge for something quick. There wasn't much other than eggs, milk and fruit the owner stocked the fridge with. She decided to make an omelet. The other two sat down at the stools tucked beneath the peninsula facing the kitchen. They weren't done grilling her.

Charisse tapped her long nails on the marble. "So you look like you got a little pep in your step. You had a good time talking to this person?"

"Yep. Her name is DeeDee. She lives here part time. Apparently, she plays for the WNBA."

"Wait a minute. The WNBA?" That bit of information seemed to trigger something for Charisse. Her brain was working overtime. "Does she happen to have locs?"

"Yes actually."

"Tall, lightish brown skin with dimples?"

Bri was thrown. "Yeah. Did you see her?"

"No. You hung out with DeeDee Renier. My niece loves her. You know who that is?" she asked, turning to Sunny. "She used to date Tori Kells from that show, 'Love, Sex and Music.'"

"Oh yeah. I remember. They got into that big public fight about Tori hanging out with her best friend."

Charisse lit up. "Do you think you can get me an autograph for my niece? Have her make it out to Leesha."

"If I run into her again I guess," she said, cracking open two eggs into a bowl.

"So," Charisse said, leaning forward. "You two were just talking the whole time?"

Bri's gut tightened, but she showed no signs of distress. "Why'd you ask like that?"

"No reason. Inquiring minds just want to know."

"Like I said. She's cool people. She actually tried to show me how to swim."

Sunny made a face. "I'm sorry what?"

"Somehow, she got me to get in the water. Now y'all know I'm scared of water."

"We know," Charisse said. "You remember that time we went to Lake Lamont on that Maine trip?"

"And she fell in the water and swore she was drowning, but it was literally knee deep."

They laughed at her expense.

"I'm not paying you two any mind. Anyway, she's motivated me to really learn how to swim and start hacking away at my bucket list." She scrambled the eggs and fetched some butter from the fridge. "I've been sitting around waiting for Q to figure out his life, while mine has been passing me by. I need to just move on. And when I say move on, I mean get back to the old me that wasn't afraid to take chances."

"Well wait a minute now," Charisse said with a hand up. "You're not gonna go jumping out of airplanes are you?"

"I don't know. Maybe." She added butter to the heated pan and poured the eggs in.

"Please don't go jumping out of airplanes. Or doing some cliche shit like cutting off your hair. Matter'fact, don't do anything drastic while you're in this state."

"Okay sis. I got it."

"But I do like the idea of you bringing back the old Bri, the one who wasn't dependent on anyone for her happiness. That probably came off wrong." She searched for words.

Sunny leaned in. "I think what she's trying to say is, you've been obsessed with this marriage thing for the last three years and it's changed you into this really..."

"Watch it-"

"-Intense individual."

"Wow. Okay. Intense. Is that another way of saying I'm uptight?"

Sunny pursed her lips. "I wouldn't say, uptight."

"I'd say uptight," Charisse said. "So I'm glad you did something spontaneous and out of character for once. Do more of that. Forget about Q, and start living your best life. Speaking of living your best life, we were thinking of going parasailing tomorrow."

"There you go with the water sports. You know I don't do water."

"Why not? It looks really fun. What happened to getting out of your comfort zone?"

"None of you can swim well enough to save me if I fall off," she said, sliding the eggs off the pan and onto a plate. "I'll go to the beach with you, but I'll be under an umbrella with my iPad."

"Ugh. You're frustrating," Charisse said, getting up from her seat. "I had so much hope for you just now. I'm going to bed. Goodnight."

Sunny stood up to go as well. "Don't listen to her. Go ahead and chop your hair off if you want to. You could pull it off."

"You think so?" Bri asked, running her hands down her braids.

"I know so. You've got the bone structure for it."

"You stay gassing me up. Goodnight ladies. Love you."

Plating her food, she gladly sat at the island to eat alone. With her phone in hand and DeeDee fresh on her mind, she set out to find her. It wasn't hard. She showed up first in a Google search for D.D. WNBA.

She clicked on the link to her Instagram account. 250k followers. Impressive. The most recent pic was a photo of her during a game, going in for a dunk. She seemed like a completely different person in that uniform doing what she does best. It only made her that more attractive. She was developing a crush on this woman and she liked the feeling.

That was posted over twelve weeks ago. She hadn't posted anything new since.

Her wall was a collage of dimpled smiles, fashion looks, new kicks, gym shots, celebs, parties, exotic places and beautiful women. She was the girl you wanted to be friends with.

Further down in the older pics, Bri noticed a string of photos that featured one woman over and over again. This must have been the Tori girl Charisse mentioned. They certainly looked good together. Bri reserved judgment other than knowing she probably wasn't the type of woman she could be friends with. Based on the way she presented herself, they wouldn't have much in common. Whether or not she respected DeeDee's choice in women, she enjoyed her company and loved her spirit. She pushed the follow button and finished her midnight meal. After a long hot shower making sure to get the chlorine out of her braids, she slipped into bed with her phone. When she unlocked it there was an

Instagram notification waiting for her. DeeDee followed her back and to her delight, also sent a DM.

I didn't know you were a lawyer.

You didn't ask. [wink emoji]

Beautiful and smart? That's just sexy AF.

Bri thought about her next response. Her pulse quickened as she texted back.

Not as sexy as you are.

She covered her face with a pillow and waited for DeeDee's response. It came back fast.

Excuse me Counselor!!! Are you flirting with me?

Maybe. [thinking emoji] Thanks for the swimming lesson btw.

The pleasure was all mine. [wink emoji]

I'm sure. Getting ready for bed?

Already in bed. But can't sleep.

Same. Slept too much earlier.

There was a brief pause before DeeDee responded again. Then:

...Facetime me. 555-413-8913.

Her heart pumped at the rate of a hummingbird's wings. If she called, she'd be crossing a line into a world she had only lived in her fantasies. You're straight Bri, she rationalized, but the body doesn't lie. She was attracted to this woman on a physical level. That much she could admit to herself. She was single again and looking for a good time, at least for the duration of the trip. She had nothing to lose.

…Okay.

FIVE

"Bri, you plan on waking up? It's damn near 10 o'clock," someone said, from the other side of her door. She opened an eye and winced from the brightness of the sun. She rolled over in her bed and buried her head under a pillow.

There was a knock at the door a few seconds later. She popped her head up and almost forgot where she was for a moment.

"Bri, we're gonna go."

She managed to sit up and drag herself out of bed. She poked her head out of the door. Kayla was dressed in a bathing suit with a leopard dress coverup.

"Oh this is cute," Bri said, with as much enthusiasm as she could muster.

"Thank you. So you're really not coming?"

Bri exhaled deeply. "I was planning to..."

Charisse came into view. "You look like shit," she said. "Did you get lit all by yourself last night?"

"Yep," she lied. "Now my head is killing me."

They shook their heads disappointed.

"Will you be okay?" Kayla asked.

"I'll be fine. Go on and have fun without me."

"Fine, but you're coming to dinner with us, whether or not we have to drag your ass out is up to you."

"I will. I promise."

She closed the door and slipped back into bed. She may as well have gotten wasted. She stayed up talking to DeeDee until about five in the morning. Which one of them fell asleep first was a mystery.

She was being a horrible friend, she could admit that. But knowing they had husbands to go back home to was a constant reminder of what it seemed she was never going to have. They had everything now, the career, husband, kids, and even though things weren't always peaches and cream, they were happy. She was miserable, and DeeDee was living in her own version of misery with that knee injury. On that, they could commiserate.

During their five hour conversation, DeeDee confided that the doctors didn't give her a good prognosis. She tore her knee three times in the same place and this time, even with therapy, they didn't think it would ever get back to the way it was. It affected her game after the first time. She didn't play as aggressively as she used to, the very thing that made her intimidating on the court.

It killed her to think about a career shift, but at thirty-two it was inevitable. It was time to rethink her life before she ate through all of her savings. She had some ideas, but struggled to commit to anything. It was hard to see herself doing anything other than basketball.

Bri in turn shared her fears. Marriage was one of those things she had on her list of desires since before she even understood it's meaning. She was a hopeless romantic, delusions fostered by the hundreds of romance books she snuck into her bedroom and read as a young girl. She wanted a whole family, the husband and then the baby, in that order and she wanted it before the clock started to run out on her.

This fear was probably instilled by her mother, who from the time she could remember told her never to come home with a baby if it's not attached to a ring and a husband. She used herself as an example, often saying life would be much easier if she had a husband to help.

Her mother was long gone now, but her expectations lingered like a ghost, always steering her to moral ground. And for what?

The girls were right. The need to fulfill this expectation within a particular window of time did leave her a little intense. Coupled with the work she did, she had little time to fool around with anyone who wasn't clear on their future.

"Maybe that's why I'm single again," she said. "I keep putting out this desperate energy because I am. Maybe I need to calm my thirsty ass down a little bit. If marriage is meant for me, then it will be. I just need to start having fun again."

DeeDee proposed knocking something else off her list.

"Roller skating. It's fun, and easy once you get the hang of it."

"What about your knee? I would think it would be hard on it."

"Nothing a couple of pain-killers can't fix."

"Okay then."

"Aye," DeeDee chanted, with her eyes half closed. "It's a plan then."

Bri was excited, maybe too excited, she thought. DeeDee agreed to meet her after her physical therapy session she just recently resumed. It would be a thirty minute drive to Fort Lauderdale so she wanted to leave sooner than later.

Digging through her luggage, she remembered everything she packed was for the beach. She got ready and dressed for a quick visit to the overpriced boutiques that were walking distance from the apartment. She bought a couple of dresses, two pairs of heels and for the day, opted for a pair of white short-shorts and an off the shoulder cotton crop top.

Once DeeDee confirmed, she made her way to the place. The Uber driver pulled up to the entrance. There was no way to miss the building. Giant roller skates were drawn across the front with the words roll, bounce, skate.

She noticed DeeDee right away who was in mid conversation with a woman who seemed to find everything she was saying funny.

With a deep exhale, she stepped out of the car and tipped the driver through the app. When she looked up again, someone else joined the conversation with DeeDee. She couldn't tell if they were friends, old acquaintances or people she just met.

As if she had awakened from a daze, she wondered why she was there to meet someone she herself just met, and not with her own friends.

DeeDee looked up and they made eye contact. She excused herself from the women and made her way over.

"Come through legs," she shouted from across the space between them. That face heading toward her was the reason she had lost her mind, that smile, that swag, that flirtatious twinkle in her eye that seemed reserved just for her. "You're looking real Miami," she said, giving her a half hug.

"That was the goal. You're looking fly too," Bri said, admiring her shirt adorned with a gold studded lioness on it.

They entered the building and she was grateful it wasn't too packed. Music blared through old school speakers and was lit up with the dimness of a seedy bar. A few people sat at the benches and table near the entrance, but the majority of the patrons were floating by on their skates in the large ring set in the middle of the room.

One young lady didn't look so smooth. Her arms were everywhere and she flapped them in the air like a drowning bird. She lost the fight and fell backwards on her ass while the other skaters moved past her like the road kill she was.

"I think maybe I'll sit this one out," Bri said, as she slipped on the size seven skates DeeDee rented for her.

"You didn't come all this way to sit it out." She stood up. On skates she seemed even more like a giant. "Alright, I'm gonna give you five minutes to get your mind right. When I get back, it's go time."

"Fine," she mumbled.

DeeDee teetered from the carpeted area to the entrance of the ring and glided into the traffic of speeding skaters. Bri watched her from the other side. She looked like a pro, dancing and dipping to the old school music.

When she came fully around, she skated up close, giving her a wink, before rolling on. When she came around again, one of the girls she was talking to outside was skating and dancing alongside her. She watched them from where she kneeled on the bench, and decided she didn't like that woman.

She was being petty, no doubt about it, but she couldn't help feeling like DeeDee was hers, at least for the time she planned to be with her. She decided not to watch, turning to her phone for the time being.

A few minutes dashed by and she had zoned out long enough to be startled when DeeDee rolled up on her.

"Are you ready?" She looked up to find DeeDee with her hand out towards her. "Come on."

Bri put her hands in hers and tried to get off her seat, but her feet rolled from under her and she dropped back down.

DeeDee coached her through the initial phase of just being able to stand on the skates. A little girl watched her on the verge of laughter the entire time. Indeed, she looked as silly as she felt, but she was no quitter. And DeeDee was so encouraging, she didn't want to quit before going around at least once.

She managed to find her balance well enough to stand and move one foot in front of the other like a robot.

"Alright, let's get you out here."

"I don't think I'm ready for that."

"Didn't I say I got you? I didn't let you drown yesterday and I won't let these people run you over. So let's get to it."

"Fine. But next time, we're doing something you're afraid to do."

"That's gonna be hard, boo. 'Cause I 'aint scared of nothin'."

"We'll see about that."

She let DeeDee guide her on to the ring while skaters whizzed by. She freaked out any time anyone got too close.

"Keep your eyes on me," DeeDee told her.

It was easy to do that, so she did. By the third go around, DeeDee let her only hold one hand. She wobbled around a bit, but she managed to keep up her own balance. There was a short moment, when she started feeling herself and her song came on and she seemed like she had it down. Her foot slipped from under her and she fell on her butt almost taking DeeDee down with her.

DeeDee helped her up. They skated a little while longer as she held onto DeeDee's waist and on their last go round, DeeDee held her from behind. Halfway around the ring, her eyes fell on the girl that was pushing up on DeeDee earlier and she gave her a half smile that was just as good as saying, 'better luck next time.'

When she'd had enough of her lesson, DeeDee offered her a ride back to the apartment. She drove a cherry red Jeep Wrangler which seemed very much like her and unlike her all the same time.

"I'm glad you forced me to do that. It was fun," she said, putting on her seatbelt.

"Forced you? Is that how you feel?"

"Okay, you strongly convinced me."

"I'll take that."

The ride back seemed really short, as they got lost in conversation.

"I'm hungry and I need to load up on carbs," DeeDee said, once she exited off I-95. "Have you ever had Haitian food? A friend put me on to it and it's so good."

"I think so. I had oxtail or something. It was kind of sweet."

"That was probably Jamaican food then. Haitian oxtail isn't as sweet. We can do Jamaican or

Haitian. I'm just in the mood for some Caribbean food."

Bri let her choose. She opted for the Haitian food since she hadn't had it in a while. The restaurant was packed with people yelling in Creole for their to-go orders. DeeDee ordered red bean rice, fried plantains and a whole fried snapper that took almost an hour to get. While they waited among the commotion, Bri's phone buzzed. A new message from Q.

Can you call me please. Need to hear from you.

It was just another half assed attempt at getting her attention. He wanted her back, but didn't want her thinking things had changed. 'Can you call me' was really code for, *'Can we just put this behind us?'*

She dismissed the message as DeeDee was busy texting on her own phone. If this were a month ago, she would've pounced on his first plea to call him. Something had changed this time. As if a light switch had been turned off and she could no longer see a pathway back to him. The trail had gone cold and she had no desire to find it.

The food aroma filled the car and just from that, she understood why DeeDee was willing to wait.

They drove to her temporary home and set up at an empty table near the pool. There were just a few other people enjoying the cool, breezy day.

DeeDee suggested they could wash their hands in the bathroom located in the lobby and with that, she was suddenly worried about running into Charisse or any of the girls. She saw their parasailing photos which were posted several hours ago. They would probably be back by this time unless they went somewhere else. It would be a bad look and she'd have a hard time explaining how she managed to find time for her, but couldn't bother making the effort for them.

By the time they were done washing up, Bri was really ready to eat.

"This is called peeklees," DeeDee said, pointing to a small container of finely cut cabbages. It's spicy, but nothing you can't handle. This is how I eat it."

She took a fried plantain, loaded some of the peeklees on it and a piece of the fish she took extra care to remove the bones from. She handed it to Bri who reached for it.

"Nope," she said. "Open up."

Bri scoffed. "You are not gonna feed me out here in front of all these people."

"The hell I won't."

Bri couldn't help but laugh. The combination of nerves and the determined look on DeeDee's face had her unraveling.

"Ahhh, open wide," DeeDee said, waving the food under her nose.

It smelled really good and at this point, she just wanted the torture to be over. She closed her eyes and once the food was in her mouth, she bit down. She chewed and kept chewing realizing she had bitten off a bit more than she could easily swallow. She covered her mouth to keep from laughing and spitting food everywhere.

"It's good right?" DeeDee asked. She nodded, and took a sip of her sugary soda trying to keep from choking. "Don't take such a big bite next time," she teased.

DeeDee stuffed her own mouth, satisfied with her ability to get her to do just about anything she wanted. As if she knew the super power of her eyes, she kept them on her and Bri did her best to compete.

She stole a plantain from her plate. "You're such a damn flirt."

DeeDee scrunched up her face. "Am I?"

"No one's ever told you that before?"

"Maybe. But I don't see it."

"Oh really. You don't see how you might come off as a flirt?"

"It's called being friendly."

"Okay. If that's what we're calling it." DeeDee leaned in close. "What?" Bri asked, feeling more self conscious by the second. DeeDee reached up and wiped something off near her lips. "Thank you. What was on there?"

"Nothing. I just wanted to touch your face."

Bri shook her head as she bubbled over with laughter. "I am so done with you."

DeeDee leaned back against her seat with a sinister grin plastered across her bright face. "I hope the hell not."

SIX

Bri pushed salad around her dinner plate and took a small bite of something green. She looked around the restaurant admiring the large pendant lights that hung over each table. It cast a golden glow over the entire room that had all of them looking like goddesses.

Even Charisse, who wasn't into a heavily made up face, did a particularly great job with her makeup, sporting a sexy cat eye and dark red lip. Sunny was a vision in yellow with her hair pulled back and Kayla went for a strapless all black dress with a split that would have her husband on high alert.

From her shopping excursion earlier in the day, she picked an eggplant colored jumpsuit with a plunging neckline in the front and back. It was the last thing she should've worn if she wanted to keep a low profile. They caused a small traffic jam as they waited at the crosswalk to get to the restaurant. Some guy in a Lamborghini stopped in the middle of the street just to watch them walk across.

The receptionist gave them one of the best booths where they could see everyone and everything going on. Some of the diners who sat at the large party table in the center struck up conversations with them. It was a good time all around, but Bri wasn't fully present.

Bri set her fork down and sipped on her wine. Her mind drifted off to thoughts of DeeDee and their day together. It wasn't a date, but it sure felt like one.

Charisse snapped her fingers. "Hello-o."

"Yes? What happened?"

"I asked you, if that's all you're going to eat?"

"Oh yeah. I'm not all that hungry. Had a late lunch," she admitted.

"Interesting."

"Is it?"

"Only because you weren't in the apartment when we got there. I was just wondering where you were."

Bri stuffed her mouth with a forkful of lettuce, nuts and bleu cheese.

"Excuse me ladies," their waitress interjected. She placed new glasses filled with their drinks on the table. Bri planned to give her a massive tip for showing up right on time to break Charisse's inquisition. "This was sent on behalf of those gentlemen over there." She pointed to a table of older hispanic men. They were smiling from ear to ear.

"Oh, okay. Guess we should thank them," Sunny said through clenched teeth. They raised their drinks in their direction as a thank you. "Let us pray this will be all they want."

It wasn't. A small band took the stage and as soon as the Salsa music started, several people hit the dance floor.

"Oh damn. One of them is coming over here," Kayla said, "and I think he's coming to me."

She was right.

"Hola," he said. He was a small guy with a great head of hair and a contagious smile.

"Come...dance salsa," he said, his voice deep and confident.

Kayla declined. "Me...no salsa. Don't know how."

"I show you," he insisted.

Another one approached Bri and she was already declining the offer. He wasn't going to give up that easily though. He made a little move with his hips and held out his hand. She laughed, but he looked good doing it.

In a moment of clarity, she changed her mind. Learning a new dance was somewhere on her list. She had already gotten a lesson in swimming, one in roller skating, and now this guy was willing to teach her a few salsa moves. Sure it would be in front of all these people, but who cares. The universe was obviously trying to tell her something.

She let him take her hand and she could see the shock in Kayla's face as the other guy continued asking her to join him. Bri shrugged and he whisked her off to the dance floor. She could tell right away, just in the way he handled her hands, that he knew what he was doing.

She had a good idea of what salsa looked like, she simply wasn't sure how well she could execute it on a first try.

He started by counting, uno, dos, tres, quarto, as he slowly led her through the steps. Other dance couples sashayed, twirled and swung around them as she did her best to follow her partner's instructions. She kept at it until they got into a groove. She was doing it and he smiled with approval.

He also took it as a sign that she could move to level two, as he made a sudden maneuver with his hips, forcing her to do a quick twirl of sorts. He brought her back in and swung himself around her. She could barely keep up with what he was doing, but somehow, she managed to look right doing it. So long as her feet and hips kept moving, he led her through the movements. He spun her around without warning and she landed back in the right spot.

She looked across the dance floor to see all her girls getting lessons in salsa as well, even Kayla. Neither of them knew what they were doing, but they looked good doing it. This was fun, she thought. But who the hell was watching their purses?

◆◆◆

They trudged into the apartment buzzed and exhausted from dancing all night. They settled in for a night of pajamas, more wine and conversation.

Bri strolled to the couch and plopped down next to Charisse. "If I knew I'd be dancing salsa tonight, I would not have worn those shoes."

"They were cute though," Sunny said. "And I'm not gonna lie. I was shocked, you hear me? Shocked...to see you get on that dance floor."

"I told you guys. I'm stepping out of my comfort zone."

Charisse folded a foot beneath her on the couch and turned to face her. "Speaking of stepping out, you never did say where you went off to earlier."

With shifty eyes and an awkward smile, Bri filled her cheeks with wine and pretended she couldn't speak because of it.

They shot glances at each other and turned their attention back to her. No words were spoken. They simply waited patiently for an answer.

"Alright. I went roller skating."

"Roller skating?" Charisse repeated, as if she almost didn't believe it. "By yourself?"

Bri's phone buzzed. Another message from Q. She shook her head. "Would you believe after a whole damn month, Q keeps texting me?"

Charisse crossed her arms. "Oh so you're just going to change the subject on us?"

"Have you answered him?" Kayla asked, taking the bait. Of all the three of them, she wanted to see them win the most.

"Why would I?" He's doing what he always does. This is the game he plays. He wants to talk in order to convince me that I'm the one that's being unreasonable. It's so crazy because I've spent so much time trying to be the perfect person so he would want to marry me. You wouldn't believe the things I've done for that man."

She cleared her throat and batted back tears. More than anything, she hated the fact that she was still so emotional about him.

"I can see clearly now though. I've been doing it for so long, I don't really know who I am or what I want anymore."

Sunny nodded. "Well, it's hard to see it when you're in it. Sometimes it takes stepping out of a bad situation in order to see it for what it is."

"Exactly. That's why I told you guys, I'm taking a break from men."

"You mean you're taking a break from relationships," Kayla clarified.

"Nope, men in general."

"Wow. You spend one night with a lesbian and you're already switching sides?"

Bri shrugged. "I hung out with her today too."

"I knew it," Charisse said, jumping out of her seat. "Give me my money," she demanded, pointing to the other two.

"Alright, alright. Settle down," Sunny said. "I'll get you your whole five dollars."

"Come with it. I told these heffas you were probably hanging out with her again. I heard you on the phone last night while I was on my way to the kitchen and I knew it wasn't Q."

Sunny shook her head. "Careful Bri," she said. "Everybody knows she's a big 'ole flirt. That's how she got Tori."

"Yes, I'm very aware." She pouted. "But she's hilarious and so easy to talk to." She picked up one of the pillows to hide her face. "And I don't know if it's her masculine energy or what, but I think she's fine as hell."

"She is though," Charisse agreed, "on a strictly hetero basis of course."

They laughed and high-fived each other, but Kayla shook her head with disapproval. It was Q or bust for her.

"Well I say do you," she said.

Bri was surprised to hear it. They all were.

"What? You're on vacation. You're allowed to be on your baddest behavior. Forgive me Lord," she said looking up and putting her hands together in a prayer pose.

"Oh my god," Bri chuckled. "Relax guys. It's a little harmless flirting. I'm just having fun. I'm not switching teams or making any declarations. I've been feeling down about myself and her attention just lifts me up a little."

In the silence that swelled between them, they seemed to accept the space she was in.

"Well, I'm glad you finally let us in, secret squirrel." Sunny raised her glass in the air for a toast and everyone followed. "Go on and get your groove back Stella."

Bri was grateful to hear it. "To new and exciting grooves."

SEVEN

She nearly fell off the couch. At some point, she dozed off in the middle of their conversation. It seemed everyone had gone to bed themselves. The lights were out and someone took the time to cover her with a blanket.

Guided by the light of the moon, she found her way to the bedroom to use the bathroom. She headed back to the living room for her phone and found it on the coffee table where she left it.

She had three messages. One of them from her paralegal/assistant who was holding down the fort for her while she escaped for the week. She was requesting access to a client file she couldn't open. Another from Q and the last one from DeeDee. Her insides clenched at the sight of her name.

She responded to her assistant and quickly moved on to DeeDee's text which was a simple:

U up? Come thru...Apt 1520.

It was sent a little over two hours ago. She was happy to know that she was on her mind as well.

She decided to call and after four rings, DeeDee picked up.

"Hey, did I wake you?"

"Yeah," she said. "I fell asleep waiting for you. I thought maybe I scared you off."

Goodness. Even her sleepy voice was sexy. "You don't scare me."

"No?" She laughed softly. "Then come over."

"It's almost two in the morning."

"You got somewhere to be later?"

"Maybe."

"Well then come over let me tuck you in."

She had already decided she would go, but she had to put on a show of resistance, one she could use to justify her actions by saying she tried.

After sending the girls a group text letting them know where she'd be, she took the elevator down two levels to the fifteenth floor. Her stomach fluttered in waves as she did her best to calm her breathing.

When she turned the corner to find the right door, DeeDee was already waiting, wearing a UCLA sweatshirt and bear printed boxers. Her heart pounded wildly at the sight of her and she knew things had gone beyond a playful crush.

DeeDee beamed as she drew closer. They hugged as though they hadn't seen each other just a few hours before.

"Welcome to my humble abode."

The apartment was set up a little differently. Having only one bedroom, the main living space was larger. She also had partial views of the city and water.

The space was a mood. The scent of vanilla wafted from somewhere in the room. R&B music, maybe Ro James, played softly in the background and the lights were turned down low enough to see the twinkling city lights.

Bri took in the space. "Really nice. I didn't expect your place to be so..."

"Feminine?"

"That's the word."

"My ex decorated it. Didn't have the energy to redo it."

The word ex rang in Bri's ears. She only assumed it was over between her and Tori. Now it was confirmed.

"She has great taste. I do love this oversized couch. Restoration Hardware?"

DeeDee nodded. "Impressive."

"In another life I think I would be an interior designer. My favorite thing to do is mall-walk into furniture stores and imagine how I would design the rooms." She walked towards the balcony. "It's crazy you get to wake up to this every morning."

"I know right. I could see myself here on a permanent basis. You want something to drink? I've got wine coolers, light beer."

"It's a little late. Do you have any wine?"

"Nope. Sorry. Don't have any bougie juice."

"Bougie juice?" Bri rolled her eyes. "Who drinks wine coolers anymore? Just give it here."

On a wall with a console table nestled against it sat several small to large trophies. Bri went over to check them out. Most of them were for basketball, MVP this and MVP that. She was a fellow high achiever, something she could easily relate to. The smaller ones were awards for philanthropic contributions with the Boys and Girls club and the Y.

She barely had any photos, save for a few that hung on the wall above.

"Is this your mom," she asked, staring at a photo of DeeDee's younger self hugging an older looking woman.

"That's my gramma. She raised me from the time I was nine."

"Mom wasn't in the picture?"

She didn't quite nod. "Something like that. Drug addiction."

"Sorry to hear that. It's not the same I know, but I lost my mom at nineteen...to cancer."

"It's a major loss either way. Look at us, two quasi-orphans."

"I know right."

She sat on the couch and looked towards the views. Next to the sliding doors stood two crutches she hadn't noticed before.

DeeDee brought her a bottle and took a sip from her own. She winced right before sinking into the couch.

"Should you be on your feet like that?" Bri asked. "Looks like you're in a lot of pain."

DeeDee took another long sip. "I'm always in pain." She slouched down into the couch resting her head against it. "It's just a shitty situation. Sometimes it feels like the universe dangles the thing you want the most in the world like a carrot in front of you."

"But has no intention of letting you have it."

DeeDee looked over at her. "Exactly."

Bri sighed. "Aren't the two of us just a bundle of joy?"

"Please. This right here was meant to be. This," DeeDee pointed to the both of them, "is divine intervention."

"Is that right?"

"You don't believe it?"

For the first time, DeeDee wasn't wearing that disarming grin. She pulled her hair up and held it there as if deciding whether or not she should say the words coasting through her mind.

Bri waited patiently.

"Last night when you showed up was the first time I had been out of this apartment in three weeks. I didn't leave for anything, not physical therapy, not even to my friend's bachelorette party...not that I wanted to go. I spent that entire day trying to talk myself into coming down to the pool and I wasn't successful until late that night. And then you showed up, like a fucking angel."

Bri scoffed. "I'm far from that."

"Yeah, I know. But it feels like it. You've been like a ray of sunshine these last two days. This feels right."

Bri swooned at her words. It was a very romantic thing to say and she liked that, the overtness. It was reassuring.

Her pulse quickened, stirred by the intimate turn of their conversation. They held each other's gaze as DeeDee moved in close, crowding her space, smelling like a cross between baby powder and the strawberry daiquiri she was sipping on.

It did feel right and there was no explaining why. Perhaps it was the alcohol coursing through her veins, or the fact that she was now fully open to the idea of DeeDee and everything she came with.

She willed her to do something. Anything. She simply didn't want to be the one to make the first move. It's easier to get swept up in the moment when someone else is driving the bus, but DeeDee wasn't going to let her skate by. It was up to her. Her actions would dictate if this went anywhere beyond kismet.

With her heart in her throat, she threw back the rest of her drink and set the almost empty bottle on the table. DeeDee watched her with one dimple on full display.

She stood up from the couch as logic threatened to derail her from the growing desire to cross the line with this woman. Without another thought, she straddled herself on top and wrapped her arms around her neck. She moved in close so her lips hovered just around DeeDee's. The electricity coursing through her was palpable as she could feel their breaths meet in the small space between them.

Chills ran through her as DeeDee's hands slid across her waist and pulled her in close.

Their lips finally met and they bounced softly against each others'. It was already everything she needed. Their tongues danced, slow and indulgent, the lingering aftertaste of their wine drinks flavoring their kiss.

Closer.

DeeDee set a hot trail of kisses down her neck as her free hand made its way down, all the way down to the roundest part of her bottom where she squeezed. Adrenaline shot through her in hot and cold bursts. They kissed with fever, as if afraid the moment would end any second.

She relished the feeling of DeeDee's hands slipping up beneath her shirt, up her stomach and beneath her breast and braced herself for the moment her fingers brushed over a pebbled nipple. She rested her forehead against hers as DeeDee massaged the sensitive bud between her fingers. "I...I've never been with a woman," she huffed. DeeDee held her face until she focused. "That's okay. You know I've got you." Sexier words had never been spoken.

Slipping her hands through her locs, she tightened her grip as DeeDee rubbed on them. She shivered when she lifted her shirt and took one of the rigid nipples into her mouth, moaned freely as DeeDee licked, sucked and nibbled on it. She watched as she handled them like two ripe juicy mangoes she had no intention of sharing.

Back and forth, she'd leave one wet and waiting while she subdued the other with her mouth. With each lick, each flick, each suckle, each nibble,

Bri unraveled a little more. She closed her eyes, bit down on her lip and reveled in the delicious sensations. The longer DeeDee paid them lip service, the more the other little nub nestled between the folds of her lower lips begged for some of that same attention.

She reached down and pulled her shirt up over her head, throwing it somewhere across the room.

DeeDee leaned back against the couch with a new expression. Bri didn't know what to think of it.

"Something wrong?"

"Not at all," DeeDee said. "I'm just taking you in."

She felt her face grow flush as DeeDee's eyes canvassed her body, from her full parted lips, to the natural concave of her neck, down past her full rounded breasts.

High on anticipation, she helped DeeDee out of her own shirt. At the sight of her ample breasts tucked in a sports bra, she was reminded all at once that DeeDee was in fact, all woman. They kissed again, hands everywhere, temperatures rising, chills.

DeeDee's hands slithered up her thighs, past her hips to her ass where she sunk her fingers into its meat. She pulled her in tight and turned so Bri was now on her back.

Surprised and a little disoriented, she giggled. DeeDee pulled her under and wrapped a gentle hand around her neck, moved it down her chest, and rested it where her heart beat at a mile a minute.

She moved past her flattened stomach and even lower down the middle of her thighs. Bri held her breath hoping she would address the throbbing situation below, but DeeDee simply retraced the path back up her body.

Bri wanted more, whatever it would be. She wrapped her legs around hers and tried to pull her in for another kiss. She missed, as DeeDee resisted. A devious smile swept across her face, a subtle message that she was the one in control and would keep her waiting for as long as she wanted to.

DeeDee lowered herself above her and set her thighs so one of them rested in between her legs. She landed soft pillowy kisses and Bri took them as they came. She almost lost herself as DeeDee moved on her, basking under the friction her thigh created as it pressed against her budding clit. Bri ran her hands through her locs that fell over her face like drapes and gripped them as they locked eyes.

It was all so simple, this friction, the kissing, this…eye contact, but it felt like everything. She vibrated all over, as if their frequencies were aligned and finely tuned in some way.

DeeDee nestled herself beside her, clearing a path to the place where Bri often pleasured herself. This time, she got right to it, sliding her hands beneath her waistband, all the way down until she covered the very thing that made her a woman. Bri let her legs fall open as DeeDee slipped a finger into her sodden slit. She was ready. Beyond ready.

She held DeeDee's gaze as her gentle hand did the work her expanding clit so readily relished. Her body responded in shivers with each stroke.

Back and forth her hand slid and Bri held onto her arm because there was nothing else to latch on to. With each shift and lick, Bri fell apart a little bit more. It was good, too good. She could feel the rise from within her, that point when the build up was so strong, it would be criminal to stop. Yet that's what DeeDee did. She stopped and for Bri, it was as if someone had snatched her off a rising cloud.

"What is it?"

DeeDee rolled over from beside her and got to her feet. She put her hand out.

"I can't use my knees for this next part. We need to move this party over to my bed."

Bri took her hand without another word. DeeDee led her down a short hall and into her bedroom. In a sudden move, she twirled Bri onto the large plush bed. She fell against the surface and before she could get her bearings, DeeDee perched herself on top.

She scooted herself back towards the pile of pillows as DeeDee followed with hunger in her eyes. Before she could move any further, DeeDee latched on to the waistband of her shorts and pulled it all the way off leaving her bottomless and fully naked.

Bri bit down on her bottom lip, smiled perhaps with too much eagerness. She inhaled and exhaled deeply to calm the new buzz running through her.

DeeDee grabbed a decorative pillow and slipped it underneath her.

This is new, she thought, but it made sense right away. Her honey pot was right where DeeDee wanted it. She had been set on a platter so to speak, to be feasted on with ease.

DeeDee's mouth was on her inner thigh now, where she rubbed her cheek against it, kissed and bit softly up to the point where Bri wanted her to really address.

She watched DeeDee position her face at the altar of her source of pleasure. She could hardly contain herself, knowing that her tongue on her clit was going to be exactly the cure for her heartbreak. Only DeeDee was intent on teasing her. She kissed everywhere around it, blew on it directly so it flourished like a budding flower. She just wanted her to get it done.

"Please," she pleaded. "I'm sorry what?"

"Can you just...?"

"Can I just what?"

Bri pouted. DeeDee found pleasure in her desperation and there wasn't much she could do about it. She was just going to have to be patient. This just wasn't what she was used to, this kind of deliberate attention to every inch of her body. She exhaled, closed her eyes and allowed herself to simply enjoy the sensations, enjoy the anticipation and build up.

It was worth the wait. The pay off came suddenly, the warmth, the wetness, the full immersion of her clit in this woman's mouth. She opened her eyes to watch DeeDee lick her from the opening of her cum soaked freshly waxed lips to the top of her thumping, swollen nub.

Her legs trembled and her blood ran hot as she yearned for more.

She licked it again and again as her clit fluttered and expanded against her hot tongue, all the while moving herself further and further into her mouth. It was the sweetest, most potent feeling, the kind of indulgence one can instantly get hooked on.

She latched onto the pillows next to her and raised her legs as high as she could, giving her renewed access. DeeDee pried her legs open as she dived in with more fever, masticating on all that was her. She put her whole face in it and it sent Bri off. It was all she needed at that point. No need for penetration. It would only distract her from her work.

She guided her to the exact spot she really wanted her to work.

"*Ffffffuck.* Yeah...yeah...yeah," she whimpered. "That-that's so good."

Unable to contain herself, she danced underneath her mouth. DeeDee followed the rise and fall of her body with ease.

When she came up for a break, her finger did the work to keep her warm and flourishing. She paused, just long enough for Bri to open her eyes and gaze down at her.

She picked up where she left off and Bri was immediately pulled back in, her heart pounding so hard in her chest she thought it would stop. She started to lose control of her movements as high pitch sex sounds flowed consistently from her.

DeeDee kept on that little nub as though she owed it something. She was floating, surfing on a wave of feet tingling, mind numbing, fervid energy that was sure to come to an explosive end. She was close, letting the rise overtake her slowly, but surely, ready to willingly drown in it.

"Oh damn. I'm coming," she said, grabbing a handful of locs she was careful not to pull on too hard.

It came like a rush, the beating pressure releasing into a wash of euphoria. Her legs that were splayed open now clenched around DeeDee's head like a vice as her back arched up away from the mattress beneath her. She bucked and danced, her toes curled, eyes rolled back, and she gasped for air as DeeDee suckled her to the finish line.

"Oh god. Don't stop. Please...don't stop," she seethed, through clenched teeth.

She rocked herself back and forth as she rode the wave up and slowly back down to a hot simmer.

DeeDee let up only when she released her grip from her hair, but didn't stop, not just yet. This part was almost just as good as the climax, when everything was still sensitive to touch, and each gentle lick still sent electricity through her.

She fell against the bed and worked at letting the air back in her lungs. New soft kisses trailed up her legs and her body trembled.

Once she caught her breath, she perched herself up on her elbows, still dizzy and high from her orgasm. As she looked at DeeDee with her face covered from her liquid release, she knew she had committed herself to something way beyond a late night romp in Miami with a beautiful stranger.

EIGHT

The smell of bacon coaxed her out of sleep. It took her a moment to catch her bearings. She was waking up in yet a new bed in the same week. She draped the sheets around her and stepped out of the bedroom. DeeDee was in the kitchen whipping up what looked like a breakfast feast.

Her head hurt. It was only nine. She could use a few more hours of sleep. Retreating back to the bedroom, she relieved her bladder, and took a long, hot shower. As she washed the sex from her body, she thought about what she undoubtedly initiated last night, all the filthy things DeeDee did to her, the long talk afterwards, dozing off in her arms only to be awakened for another go. The very thought of it made her feel flush all over again.

She swished her mouth with a bit of Listerine as she wiped the fog from the mirror. Feeling fresh and invigorated, she stared at her reflection unsure of the woman looking back at her. Whoever she was, she liked what she saw.

DeeDee was plating a waffle when she waltzed into the kitchen.

"You went crazy in here," she said, looking at the spread. She leaned in for a kiss. One peck, two pecks, and then it got hot and heavy.

DeeDee broke away to focus on the grill. "Go on now. You almost made me burn this waffle," she said.

"What is all this?"

"You got some waffles made from scratch, turkey bacon, some potato hash and I'm about to make the eggs."

"Who's gonna eat all this food?"

DeeDee surveyed the damage. "Okay. I might've gone a little crazy."

"Charisse would tear this up though."

"Then invite her over."

"I'm sorry what?"

"You heard me. Invite them over."

Bri shook her head. "I don't know about that."

"Why not?"

She wasn't sure. It wasn't so much about what went down between them last night. There wouldn't be any judgment coming from them. In a way, she had their blessing...a vacation hoe pass so to speak. Besides that, the girls would appreciate it. They spent a lot of time taking care of and cooking for their families. They always loved it when someone else cooked for them.

DeeDee didn't seem to care either way. "Just ask them. Doesn't hurt."

She took a deep breath and found her phone to make the call.

"Hey Reece."

"Who's this?" Charisse asked.

"Stop playin'. You know it's me. What are you doing right now?"

"I'm just getting ready to take a shower."

"If you're up to it, DeeDee made a huge breakfast and she wanted me to invite you guys over."

There was silence on Charisse's end. There was no telling what was running through her mind.

"You spent the night over there?"

"Yes," Bri whispered, looking over at DeeDee. "I sent you a text saying so." She braced herself for a scolding.

Charisse laughed. "Girl, I thought you were calling me from your room. Alright. I'll tell Kay and Sunny."

Bri hung up pleased with how easy that task turned out to be.

"Looks like they're coming which means you probably have to make more of everything. They'll probably be a while though because Charisse takes forever."

"No problem. We've got this."

"What do you mean we?"

The waffles were kept warm in the preheated oven. DeeDee had her follow a recipe on how to make syrup. Although the steps were simple, it was an intimidating process.

"Who makes syrup from scratch?"

"I hardly keep anything processed in the house. If I want something bad, I either have to go out to get it or I have to make it. Keeps me in check."

"Ew. You're so...disciplined and stuff."

"I always thought that was a good thing."

"It is. It's hot actually."

DeeDee shot her a warning look. "You keep saying stuff like that, I might have to put you on this counter and have you for breakfast."

"You keep saying stuff like that, I might just let you."

Sexual energy was in the air and it was intoxicating. Her heart raced and the nub nestled between her thighs peaked when it was clear DeeDee had all the intentions on following through.

The knock at the door sucked her right out of the moment. They were there much sooner than she expected. Letting out a calming deep breath, she let the girls in and quickly introduced them to DeeDee who told them to make themselves at home. They seemed to take an instant liking to her, complimenting her on the decor and discussing her trophies.

She helped DeeDee set up the spread at the kitchen island. They moved around each other with a familial ease. Charisse noticed, judging by the smile creeping across her face as she watched them. Bri gave her the stink eye in hopes she wouldn't make any of it a big deal. But that wasn't her style.

They gathered to serve themselves. "Is this a strawberry compote?" Sunni asked.

"That's what they called it in the video," DeeDee said.

Bri lifted a metal cup. "I made the syrup from scratch. Just thought I'd mention that."

Kayla seemed truly impressed. "Okay then Barefoot Conteesha. I see you. All of this looks so good. Thanks for inviting us."

The girls sat at the small four seater table DeeDee had set up by the living room and Bri sat with her on the stools.

Charisse munched on a piece of bacon. "So when does the new season start?" she asked DeeDee.

Bri felt instantly defensive for her, but DeeDee didn't seem to mind the question.

"Preseason starts in April, but I won't be ready by then."

"Why not?"

"I got injured while playing in Germany. Hell, whether I'll ever play again is still up for debate."

The room went cold. Charisse grimaced and the silence was deafening.

"I was reading about this a while back," Sunny said, coming to the rescue. "Don't you guys get paid more playing overseas?"

"Pretty much."

DeeDee was a grown woman who could handle herself, yet Bri worried they were picking at a sore wound. This was on her. She should've warned them. Charisse had more to say and she could only hope it would be about something other than basketball.

"My niece wants to play ball, like you," she said. "She's a big fan by the way. I think she follows you."

"Bet. Give me her *at* when you get a chance and I'll follow her back."

"She'd love that. Make sure you tell her Aunt Reece hooked that up."

"Will do."

"I wanted to ask you though. My sister doesn't want her going for the WNBA because like Sunny said, it's a well known fact they don't pay."

DeeDee nodded. "A lot of the players barely make forty a year," she said, stuffing her mouth with a piece of strawberry smothered waffle.

"Damn. That's worse than I thought."

DeeDee chuckled.

Charisse was never the type to hold her tongue. Bri widened her eyes in her direction, a silent signal to stop while she was ahead.

"True. I get paid better than most, but I still go overseas. I want to be able to do more than just pay bills. I have investments I want to make, a retirement to fund so yeah...I take the extra games."

"I can't imagine it's good for your body," Kayla chimed in. "When do you get a break?"

"It is hard. But we do what we've gotta do."

Bri wanted them to stop grilling her about it. In some way, they were both hurting emotionally, but DeeDee's pain was also physical.

"So what would you suggest to my niece? She's a senior in highschool right now and she's really trying to do the professional basketball thing. My sister's about ready to have a heart attack."

"If you asked me a year ago, I would've told you to tell her to consider other options. But if she's really good, you could tell your sister to do some research on it. She'd be pleasantly surprised at the changes they're making. Better pay for the best of the best,   maternity   leave,   better   travel accommodations..."

"That's good to know.." Charisse whipped out her phone. "I hope you don't mind. I'm about to fangirl on you. Can we take a pic together?"

"Of course," DeeDee said, slipping from her seat. "Got me feeling like a real somebody out here."

Bri watched the scene as if she were outside of her body. She liked this woman. It was too soon to have these thoughts, crazy even. But she could see her future and DeeDee was in it, however unrealistic it seemed at the moment.

Once everyone had their fill with breakfast, they helped clean up and thanked DeeDee for having them over. Charisse invited her to dinner. They'd be checking out Dolores in Brickell.

"Thanks, but I have an event to check out in Wynwood. A friend of mine is revealing a new mural she painted. Have you guys been?"

"I've heard about it," Sunny said.

"What? How have you never gone down there? They've turned that whole area into a massive street art gallery. You should definitely come through. It's an Instagram gold mine and the food scene is good too. If you guys are down, we can roll together."

They hadn't planned much for the day other than a little shopping and hanging out at the beach. Kayla and Sunny were game.

"I'm down for a day of arting," Bri said, as DeeDee wrapped her arms around her from behind. Charisse laughed. "What the hell is arting?"

"You don't know nothin' about that. Arting is the art of doing art things," she snipped.

"Oh okay." Charisse looked at them with a knowing smile. Bri could see her mind bubbling over with mischief. She wanted the tea, all of it, but she would have to wait. "Arting it is."

NINE

It was as if they had stepped into a new universe. Building after building boasted colorful, strange and wild pop art that screamed for their undivided attention. They walked down the sidewalk admiring the work.

Sunny was particularly enamored with a large pink building with a little girl drawn on it. A large tree sat on top of the wall creating the illusion of actual hair. They all agreed it looked just like her youngest daughter Rya. She dug up an old Instagram photo of her. It was freakishly uncanny. She took a photo and created a side by side image she posted on her page.

DeeDee was giving them a full on art tour. Earlier, she had them check out the RC Cola Plant, an abandoned building tagged with graffiti that had been revitalized into a prime event space. Then brought them to the Warehouse gallery which featured modern and vintage art. Bri loved the immersive nature of the work. You could walk in through, go beneath or even touch some of the pieces.

The Unicorn Factory was also a hit, room after room of a cacophony of colors, bubbles, and unicorns everywhere.

"We've got to bring the girls here next year," Kayla suggested, just as soon as a five year old girl started screaming that she didn't want to leave. Her mother was dragging her to the door. They watched the scene, feeling bad for the woman.

DeeDee thought it was hilarious. Kayla did not. "On second thought, she said, "I'm good."

They walked from colorful block to colorful block for a while until DeeDee suggested they make a stop at a beverage shop covered in it's own over the top design of bubbles and leaves. She treated them to some authentic bubble tea.

While they rested their feet, DeeDee tapped away on her phone.

"When's your friend's art reveal happening?" Bri asked.

"I'm going to meet up with her right now, actually. The reveal will be in about forty-five minutes."

"Then just shoot us the location. We'll catch up," Sunny said. She wanted to take a few more selfies and photos of the buildings.

"Bet. I'm gonna steal this one though," DeeDee said, referring to Bri. "You guys don't mind do you?"

"You can take her so long as you return her in one piece," Kayla said.

"I'll take care of her. I promise."

Charisse sipped loudly through her straw. "I bet you will."

Bri pinched her under her arm as she got up from her seat.

"Ouch. What was that for?"

"You know damn well."

Charisse gave her the evil eye. "Come on ladies," she said, taking her bubble tea with her. "I will not stand for this abuse."

They left the cafe going in opposite directions. "Your friends are hee-larious," DeeDee said.

"They are. Especially Reece. She keeps me on my toes, that one."

"I think my friends would like you too. They're a little more cynical and they'd put your feet to the fire, but you're smart. They're suckers for a smart chick."

"You're already thinking about introducing me to your friends?"

"Why not? I met yours."

Bri's heart skipped a beat. "Touché."

They walked down yet another colorful corridor of painted expressions. The sun beat down on them so Bri was grateful she wore a hat. Without warning, DeeDee took her hand and crossed the street with her. She followed taking extra steps just to keep up with her long strides.

DeeDee held onto her hand even when they got to the other side. Bri squeezed, so it was clear she didn't want her to let go either.

Sex was an intimate act, but for her, it was always these simple signs of affection that truly marks the state of a relationship.

A small crowd had gathered around a building toward the end of the block. It was covered with a large white cloth so no one could see beneath it.

"There she is," DeeDee said, strolling up to a young woman wearing a colorful head wrap.

"Oh shit. Who is this? Is Ms. Dorothy Divine back from the dead?"

"Wait a minute." Bri stopped dead in her tracks. "So your name is Dorothy Divine?"

DeeDee shot her a sheepish smile, but kept moving. "Didn't I say that?"

Bri lagged behind with her arms crossed. Something as important as a name was not to be played with. She had laughed so hard and now felt bad about it.

She watched them embrace like old friends do when they haven't seen each other in too long. "I'm glad to see you out and about again. What dragged you out of your hiding hole?"

"You know I wouldn't miss this."

"Well you missed the bachelorette party." DeeDee looked away for a moment, but had no words. "Relax. I get it. Believe me. She was supposed to be your friend. No one's faulting you for staying away. Hell, you're a bigger person than I am." Her eyes darted over to Bri. "So who is this?"

"My bad. This is Bri. A close friend. Bri, this is Denise, AKA Denise the Arteest. She's brilliant at what she does."

Bri gave her a cautious smile. "Nice to meet you."

"Close friend you say?" Denise studied her with a quick scan. "I love everything going on with this face," Denise gestured with her hands. It should be on canvas hanging on someone's wall somewhere."

Bri was flattered. Many things had been said about her looks, but it needing to be on Canvas, was a first. She barely got a chance to respond when Denise shifted back to DeeDee. "You sure know how to pick 'em."

DeeDee's smile only grew more strained. Denise narrowed her eyes at her like a suspicious cop. "Have you called her?"

"No. And I don't plan to."

"I think you should. More for you than her."

Bri tried to keep up with the back and forth, but there were too many missing details.

"Don't see the point in calling," DeeDee said, "but I'll think about it." She shifted her weight in her Jordans and looked toward the covered wall. "So, how's this going?" she asked, eager to change the subject.

"We're almost ready. It's so crazy I got to do this."

"I know. I remember when you said you wanted to see your art here and look at you now. You've made it! Your very own...wall."

Denise punched her in the arm. "I'm not dealing with your shenanigans today. She's a fool," she told Bri.

"I'm starting to see that."

"Anyway, thank you for being here. I have to say hey to a couple of people before we get started. Stick around so I can get some pics with you Dee."

"I'll be here," DeeDee said, while texting the location info to Bri. She sent it off to the girls then stood before her fling thing with her arms still crossed.

"What?"

"Dorothy Divine?"

"Oh right." She laughed. "It's both my grandmother's names put together. I have a thing about it."

"Okay. I get it. I'm a little upset that you kind of lied about it though."

"I'm sorry. I'll find a way to make it up to you."

"Good. Also, it sounds like there's some unfinished business with the ex."

DeeDee pulled her in close by the waistband of her shorts. "It's complicated."

"You don't have to explain anything to me. I just want to know what I'm getting into.

DeeDee lowered herself so they were at eye level.

The sun lit her eyes up so they seemed almost translucent. "Well that would only matter if you're trying to get into something."

She was so close, Bri expected a kiss to follow.

"Well, well, well." Bri swung around to find Charisse and the girls strolling casually towards them. "We're here" she sang, sipping loudly at the last bit of bubble tea in her cup. It should've been thrown away at least twenty minutes ago.

She could take Charisse's antics, though she appreciated how Sunny and Kayla did their best to appear oblivious. They didn't find pleasure in her discomfort like Charisse did. She was being as the kids say, a little extra.

The reveal ceremony started shortly after their arrival. A good crowd of a hundred or so gathered. There were two photographers snapping photos of the event. One of them gestured for them to cluster for a quick pic.

Denise made a little speech about the work and the white curtain came down dramatically, landing in a giant pool of fabric.

"Wow," the audience murmured. A round of applause soon came after.

"That is beautiful," Bri said, truly taken by the image of a woman painted in solid black. She wore all white, amidst the background of a white washed landscape. On her shoulder was the world she held with little effort. Tiny sparks of light surrounded her so she seemed to glow even in the daylight.

The starkness of the mostly black and white mural stood out against the rainbow of colors that surrounded it.

Bri made sure to tell Denise how much she loved it.

"It's political and poetic all at once."

"Well damn. I like that. I like her," she directed at DeeDee. "Bring her around the gang, you know, when things cool off."

There was so much to unpack with that, but Bri took it as a stamp of approval.

After DeeDee greeted a few other friendly faces they made their way back to the car with plenty of time left in the evening. She was kind enough to take them to Target so they could pick up some items before driving them back to their home away from home.

They thanked her for the day of what would be forever known as arting.

Before Bri could make her way out, DeeDee latched onto her hand. "I'll catch up," she told them.

Bri closed the door and turned in the seat to face her. "What's up? You've got something to say?"

"I just wanted to tell you that I like you in my space." Bri smiled hard. Too hard. "I was thinking, maybe you'd like to come up so we can um...do some things."

Although the idea of ditching her friends again didn't sit well, she had been waiting all day for the next opportunity they could be alone together.

"What kind of things did you have in mind?"

DeeDee's eyes slid down to her cleavage. "I'd rather show than tell."

She was instantly charged up by the idea. DeeDee pulled her in by the chin and she braced for impact. She had never wanted a kiss so badly.

It never came. DeeDee pulled away from her suddenly. "Well you'll have to wait. I have some errands to run."

Bri sucked her teeth. "You play too much."

"I know. I'm just messin' around. But for real. Swing by later."

"I'll have to think about it. I've got some client work to finish up and I really haven't spent enough time with my girls so..."

"Aw. She's petty," DeeDee teased.

Bri stepped out and closed the door behind her. She switched her hips as she walked toward the doors leading to the lobby.

"Damn girl. I like the way you walk away," DeeDee yelled through the window. Bri turned only halfway, but she kept it moving. "Don't make me come and find you."

Her friends were laughing and loud about it. She could hear them from the other side of the door. There were two times in high school when she didn't make it home at her at 10 o'clock curfew. The dread she felt the moments before she stepped into the house to deal with her mom was the same level of dread she was feeling now.

The minute she stepped into the apartment, all chatter stopped and all eyes were on her. They were all in the kitchen as usual and were shooting each other glances.

"Well hello there Ms. Davis," Charisse said.

"Hey ladies."

"Don't hey ladies us," Sunny said, waving a plastic cup in the air. "Have a sit in the hot seat honey cause you've got some esplainin' to do Lucy." She knew this was coming. She could hold them off, but for so long.

Kayla gave her a pleading stare and took her by the hand. "Charisse is convinced something went down between you two. Please tell me all you did was talk."

Bri's eyes shifted to all of them. The expression on her face said everything they needed to know.

"Oh lord! She dun' gone over to the other side," Kayla wailed, with her hands in the air. She held herself and hummed an old negro hymn type of song.

"Kayla you're a mess girl," Charisse said, doubled over in laughter.

Bri felt no shame about it. "Honestly you guys. I don't even know what's come over me."

Sunny bit on a finger nail and squinted her eyes at her. "Speaking of come, how many times did you?"

Bri covered her face so they wouldn't see how hard she was smiling.

"Ewww, don't wanna hear it. La-la-la-la. Don't wanna hear it," Kayla sang, making her way to her room. "If I get hot and bothered hearing these details, I may as well have done the deed myself. Lord help me. Ya'll can talk when I shut the door."

Turns out Sunny and Charisse were far more interested than she expected. They huddled around her as she took a seat at the bar stool tucked at the island.

"Spill it bitch," Charisse demanded.

"She told me to come through, so...I came through."

"And?"

"We talked."

"And?"

"And...I came about five or seven times. I lost count."

They seemed taken by this information, as if they got their own sordid satisfaction just to hear it.

Charisse sighed and chugged down some water. "See, I haven't been properly fucked since Kenneth had that car accident last year that messed up his back, so I am living vicariously through you right now."

"Gotta hand it to you," Sunny said. "You have been surprising the hell out of me this whole damn trip. Never in a million years did I think this would be you right now."

"I know. And when I tell you, the whole thing...it felt so right. And I'm not talking about the fact that she's obviously a woman. I mean, that's probably why it feels so easy. I have no guards up, no expectations, no demands, no wall and she made me feel like I had never really made love until last night."

"Are you saying you're in love?"

"No. Not at all. I can't be. Right?"

Charisse and Sunny looked at each other.

"That's that lesbian curse. I heard they fall in love easily," Charisse said.

"Is that right?"

"It makes sense. Women get each other and when we click, we click. If we weren't saddled with all these sexual and societal barriers, half of us would be sleeping with our best friends."

Sunny scoffed. "You would never."

Charisse didn't say anything, but she pursed her lips and looked toward the ceiling.

Bri's eyes widened. "No way. Charisse...you?"

"It was a threesome, junior year, with Darius."

"What?" Bri was beside herself. "You never told me."

"I didn't think you guys would be cool with it. You know sister Mary Francis over there definitely wouldn't. Anyway, a spontaneous drunken threesome isn't a night of lesbian lovemaking though. What you did is completely different."

She was right. Getting caught up in a moment was an entirely different beast. With DeeDee, it was a sober decision after sober decision to be in her presence. What happened last night was not a mistake. She was of full sound and mind when she signed that lover's contract with a kiss and sealed it with DeeDee's lips on her clit.

"Just remember, you're in Miami on vacation," Charisse added. "In three days, this fantasy is all that it will be. Don't get caught up."

Words of wisdom. But what she was feeling was already beyond a budding crush. What would become of them when it was time to go home and get back on the billable hours grind? What were the chances they could turn a vacation fling into a successful long distance relationship? Would DeeDee even want that for herself?

She wished none of it had to end and perhaps that meant she was probably too far gone. If she was in fact falling for DeeDee, it was fast and confusing, scary and exhilarating all at once.

She dismissed the racing thoughts. For as long as she could help it, she was going to keep it light and she was going to keep it fun. Whatever it turned out to be, it would be.

TEN

The sun came up and lit the bedroom with a bright white light. It washed over the two of them lighting DeeDee's face. Her skin was unbelievably clear, probably due to her diet. Bri thought she might actually give the no processed food thing a try.

She hadn't planned to end up in DeeDee's bed again, not so soon at least. After what DeeDee pulled in the car, she had all the intention to make her pay. Ms. Davis likes a tease and she can take a joke, but she is not to be made a fool, no matter how funny it is.

At about eleven in the evening, DeeDee sent her first text:

Left my door unlocked. Come thru.

Can't. Busy.

She wasn't. She was done with client work, had showered and was tucked in bed strolling through Tiktok. Although her coldness was meant to punish DeeDee, she felt as though she was punishing herself. Still, she was determined to teach her a lesson.

Half an hour later came the second message, but this time, it was sent in video. Curious, she pushed the play button.

It was a close up of DeeDee's mouth and she was munching on what looked like a plum. Some of it had been eaten, leaving some of the pit exposed.

She slurped on it, made a circle around it with her tongue and sucked on the juicy flesh of the fruit. She ate the whole thing as if she hadn't eaten in days. Once it was done and her face was completely wet with its nectar, she pulled the phone out so Bri could see her whole face.

"That could be you," she said. "Come get your blessings."

Kayla caught her as she was on her way out. Bri gave her a tight smile. "Love you. Later."

"I'm gonna pray for you," she said, through a deep yawn.

She was down there in less than five minutes. The door was unlocked. She let herself in and found DeeDee on her way to her room. No words were spoken, just the removal of clothes and the expectation of being devoured like that plum.

She pulled her into the bedroom and pushed DeeDee against the bed. She fell freely laughing a little too hard.

"What do you think you're doing?"

"You," Bri said, with a wicked grin sweeping across her face.

DeeDee sat up and pulled her onto the bed so she fell on top of her and in one fluid motion was on top of her, effectively pinning her to the bed.

"No ma'am. I do the doing."

Bri shook her head. "It's my turn," she said, but DeeDee was a lot heavier than her and she couldn't get free. "Are you serious right now?"

DeeDee positioned herself between her legs and lowered herself to steal a kiss. And then she was at her neck, nipping at her ears, peppering kisses across her chest. As much as she wanted to return the favor, she gave up easily, relishing the physical affection of this woman that already felt so familiar to her body.

She breathed into the sensation of her tongue dragging across her breast, teasing her nipples until they were hard as rocks, sucking on them until they seemed to be reaching a climax of their own. She held onto her face as she worked them and all she could think about was how glad she was to have allowed this goodness to occur.

She moaned a song of pleasure as DeeDee introduced her hand below. Her pussy weeped and her clit grew full and obedient to her caress as she kissed her slow and deep.

"Oh damn." She whispered incoherent things as her fingers entered and she slid her entire hand in and out of her, building the pressure against that little nub where it mattered most. She didn't know hands could do this. Just hands, with the right kind of pressure, the right amount of friction over and over again.

She couldn't believe it, how quickly the whole thing began to build.

Oh my god.

Her breathing gave her away, she was coming, and it was coming hard and this was the opportunity DeeDee took to make her way down there, put her mouth on it, sucked her softly,

whipped her up from the inside, had her calling her name, yanking on the sheets, pinching her own damn nipples, bucking and winding to the rhythm of her hot tongue. "Oh my god that's so good. Right there. Fuck."

DeeDee played up the sound effects. She ate loudly, humming, smacking, moaning vibrations on her ever expanding clit. It was everything and the visuals only played up the experience. She was fully worked up, DeeDee was actively fucking her world up and as the heat spread from her center onto every inch of her body, she worried that maybe this woman had ruined sex for her. This was crack as far as she was concerned and she knew better than to do drugs.

The climax hit her hard, shut her jaw and eyes down tight, had her ass high up in the air, as DeeDee sucked her down to the finish.

"Oh fuck. Oh shit, I'm coming. Don't stop, don't stop. *Fuck you, I'm coming.*"

Her legs trembled beneath her before collapsing. DeeDee released her and in that quiet moment, as she chased her own breath, they smiled wistfully at each other. They had crossed that line for the second time and then a third and forth after that, the line that automatically had her wondering about the next phase of the relationship. It only made sense. She didn't ever give it up so easily. It took five months of work for Q to see her naked. Casual sex just wasn't a part of her vocabulary and maybe that was her problem.

As she watched her sleep, she thought, I could actually, genuinely fall for this woman, beyond the idea of her and she couldn't understand why that didn't scare her more. Was this desperation, a need to cling on to something new just so she could stop feeling for the old? Or was there something real here, something that could be built on beyond this short vacation from real life.

DeeDee stirred under the sheets and fought against the light. She finally opened her eyes to find Bri staring at her. She rolled over laughing hysterically. "What are you doing?"

"Nothing. Just watching you sleep."

"That's creepy as fuck, but it's cool. I took some pics of you while you were sleeping."

"I knew you were batshit crazy."

"Oh yeah?" DeeDee attacked her with tickles.

"No, stop," she begged between uncontrollable laughter.

DeeDee pulled her in close. "Good morning, beautiful."

Bri wrapped her arms around her neck and studied the contours of her face. "Damn," she whispered. "The way you look at me."

DeeDee reached over and gave her a lingering kiss before showering her face with a hundred more pecks. It tickled.

Bri loved the playful nature of her affection, basked in the warmth and the butterflies and the dopamine it unleashed. This was sunshine on your face goodness, riding top down on Saturday afternoon goodness, dancing barefoot in the rain goodness. She wanted to stay there, just right there, in that moment forever.

"You hungry?" DeeDee asked.

"I could eat. But don't go cooking up a buffet again."

DeeDee rolled out of bed and grabbed a tank top and shorts from the dresser. "And what do you have planned for the day?"

Bri propped herself up on an elbow.

"We were planning to hang out at Lincoln Road Mall, do a little shopping, maybe hit up Cameo later."

"Oh yeah? I know the owner's girlfriend. It's a weeknight so I could probably hook you up with VIP."

"I see. You taught her how to swim too?"

DeeDee laughed out loud. "No. She already knows how to." She got dressed and slipped her locs into a rubber band so it sat on top of her head. "On a serious tip though, can I borrow your professional time for a minute?"

Bri was intrigued. "I'm on vacation, but I think I can carve out some time. My rates are $300 an hour."

"Wow. Okay. I think I can swing that, but I was hoping I built in some credit, you know, for the work I put in last night and all through the early morn'," she said with a body roll.

"So you want to cash in your chips?"

"Yeah. Just want to run some ideas by you, pick your brain a little."

Bri could see she was serious. She was flattered too, that DeeDee wanted her opinion on what was obviously an important matter.

"Guess I should go get ready then. Give me an hour."

"Works for me. Meet me downstairs in the lobby."

Quickly, she slipped out of the apartment and headed back to get ready for the day, doing a quick job of showering and getting dressed. She couldn't get it all done fast enough. Slipping on her espadrilles, she took a long look at herself in the floor length mirror only realizing the buzz that had been running through her the entire time. She really liked this woman.

The realization settled on her softly.

"Aubrinna Rae. What do you think you're doing?"

She had no answers for herself. There was no real thought behind her actions, just good feelings. That's all she wanted to lean on for now.

◆◆◆

If ever there was a day to be lounging on the beach it was today. They rode with the windows down and HER serenading them on the radio.

DeeDee hummed to the song and Bri liked the fact that it was on key. A bad voice was one of her biggest turn offs. Not that she was a song bird herself, but she felt there was no excuse for making up your own notes on a song one supposedly knows.

The words took her back to their late night session, where DeeDee did nothing, but 'focus' on her. The woman had already earned her Masters in pleasuring her, but she had yet to be allowed to reciprocate. She thought at first, she simply hadn't been clear about her intentions, but DeeDee didn't necessarily leave room for her to take control, especially last night. She wondered when she'd get the chance to and feared all at once, if she'd be able to successfully satisfy her.

"So you're not gonna tell me where we're going? What if you're driving me to a trafficking ring where I have to work as a sex slave until they're done with me?"

DeeDee eyed her curiously. "You sure that's not a fantasy?"

Bri swatted her across the arm as DeeDee laughed at her own joke. "Just sit tight. We're almost there," she assured.

They drove for a few more minutes towards Downtown. Bri perched herself outside of the window watching birds soar against a cloudless blue sky. She fought the urge to whip out her phone and take a snapshot of something, but thought against it. Not everything needed to be shared for the sake of sharing. She'd rely on good old memory for this moment. Whenever she heard this song, no matter how long it's been, she'd remember this exact moment.

"Here we go," DeeDee said, pulling into a parking lot with a two story building. It looked somewhat abandoned. The grass was dead save for a few wild bushes that surrounded the entrance. On the property adjacent to it sat a BMW dealership and on the other side a Thai restaurant.

She pulled up into a parking space and stepped out. Bri followed her to the entrance making sure not to step on the cracks.

DeeDee fiddled with several keys at the door. "You okay?"

"Yeah, just don't remember which one is the right fucking key."

"Here, let me try."

DeeDee relinquished the keys and paced behind her. Bri figured it out on the second try. She opened the door and walked into the dusty, empty space.

It had a damp smell, like that of standing water. One of the walls had a huge hole in it with the wires hanging out.

"What is this?"

"I bought it...a while back."

Bri was surprised to hear it. She looked around the space and then back at DeeDee who now held her hands behind her head. "I bought it, and now I'm freaking out about it."

"Okay. And you wanted me to see it-"

"-So you can tell me if my idea is stupid or not."

"Got it. Shoot."

"Alright," she said, shaking out nerves. "I would like to launch my own clothing line. I've got a lot of followers at this point and they're always telling me how much they like my personal style. I designed a t-shirt last year and made 500 available on my website. Sold out in a day. I figured I should really give it a serious go."

"Okay. Sounds like you've proven the viability of your business. That's a good thing."

"Yes, but I have this building though, which has been sitting here doing nothing. Then I thought, hello, this would be a great flagship store. What do you think?"

Bri walked around the massive room. There was an office to the right and a bathroom that had seen better days to the other side. Further back was a large empty room. It could've been a kitchen or a billiards room. It was unclear. The stairs seemed rickety so she didn't bother climbing it.

This is a big place in a really prime space. Must've been expensive."

"I've got a couple of investors. They fronted some of the money and I've sunk pretty much all of my savings."

Bri wanted to tell her that it was a great idea, to go for her dreams and do what her heart desires, but such lies went against her nature. She got paid very well to keep people from making bad business deals and this woman was in need of her help.

"Running a brick and mortar clothing store is expensive and hard to maintain. You need a lot of foot traffic to make enough sales just to cover the mortgage." DeeDee placed her hands on her hips and looked toward the ceiling. "So this was a bad buy?"

"Not necessarily. Real estate is a good play if you go about it right. For example, you probably can use this for your clothing, but only as a pop up shop. Once you're sold out, you move out and rent it out to someone else who could use it to do their own pop-up shop...or any event. There's enough parking space for that. What was this before?"

"A restaurant and bar I think. They took everything out though."

"So there might still be a liquor license on it. Find out."

DeeDee looked at the space as if she were seeing it for the first time. Bri could see she was open to the idea.

"So that's my advice. Sell your clothing primarily online, through your site, whichever works best, and turn this space into an event venue."

"Right. Okay." She bit on her bottom lip and clasped her fingers so tight they almost lost their color. "So all of this isn't so crazy?"

Bri shrugged. "Anybody who chooses to go into business for themselves is crazy. I would know. This is a big space and it's gonna take alot to make it what it needs to be."

"I know, but I've got a couple of friends with skills that can help."

"Friends doing you favors won't cut it. You need this done and you need it done fast. Every day it sits in this condition is money you're losing." DeeDee ran her hands through her hair and grabbed a fistful. "Hey. It's overwhelming, I know, but you asked for my opinion and I just want to make sure you know what you're getting yourself into."

"Right."

"Listen," Bri said, approaching her. "I can help with all the legal stuff, incorporation, contracts, even grants and loans, whatever you need. And um, if you're looking for more investors, I might just know someone who would be interested."

"In this place or the clothing line?"

"Doesn't matter. If the numbers make sense, I'm in."

DeeDee smiled finally. She wrapped her arms around her. "Really? For real-for real?"

"I'd have to see an official business proposal first. And if I like what I see then I would seriously consider it."

DeeDee held her face in her hands. "You do realize we've known each other for a hot second right?"

"I have to keep reminding myself of that."

"Thank you. I am definitely more scared than ever, but now that I'm fucking a brilliant business attorney, I can sleep at night. I told you this is divine intervention."

Bri was starting to believe that herself, at least she wanted to. It would explain whatever this was.

DeeDee tugged on her braids so she was forced to look up at her. "Know what else is divine?"

"What?"

"These lips." They kissed, softly, sweetly, as if they didn't have a care in the world. Bri felt the butterflies and the rush and the pounding of her heart all at once. There was no way this strong physical reaction was healthy.

DeeDee walked her backwards until they bounced against a wall and they felt up each other with the knowledge that anyone passing by might be able to see them.

"We...we can't do that here," Bri said, as DeeDee started to bring up the hem of her short sundress.

"Yeah we can. I'll keep it simple."

She cupped the bare part of her ass cheeks and Bri let her pull her under with soft pecks on her face trailing down her neck. DeeDee tugged at the thong that sat in the crack of her ass and pulled it to the side so it no longer covered her lady parts properly. The part that held her crotch felt moist and warm against her inner thigh.

DeeDee rubbed on her tits as she slithered fingers against her sodden slit.

"Damn. You're already wet." She enjoyed that revelation. "How long have you been thinking about this?"

"Only since we've been here," Bri huffed.

She lowered herself using the wall as her anchor and held on to DeeDee's strong arms as she began using her whole hand to rub on her tender clit. It purred under her soft stroking and DeeDee kissed her just as softly.

As her stroking grew stronger, so did their tongue work. She bit into her bottom lip and DeeDee winced from the pain. It only turned her on.

More pressure, faster, Bri moaned and her voice echoed through the vacant space. It was hot, sweltering even, but that only added to the heat DeeDee was generating through her. She entered her, two or three fingers maybe, and she slipped in and out, fucking her with purpose and determination.

Growing weaker by the second, she latched onto her shirt, twisted it into her fist, and forced herself to make full on eye contact with her seducer. Their lips hovered, but they only exchanged harried breaths of one sided pleasure.

Faster, her hands moved with ease across her saucy clit and back in, all the way in. With every stroke, DeeDee hit something that made her shiver like a bell as she reverberated from the inside. She let out a sound for each stroke until the rise started to take over.

"Oh god, I'm coming," she blurted, evidenced by her inability to control her lower half. DeeDee managed to keep her steady while working her to the finish.

"Oh shit, oh shit, oh shit!"

DeeDee was relentless, keeping the rhythm she had built for the last couple of minutes. Her body seized under the unyielding friction. All the hairs on her body stood up, her breath caught in the back of her throat, her legs gave out and she let out a whimper as the release overtook all of her senses. She shuddered at the finish, letting out a string of expletives that made DeeDee laugh.

She rested her head against the wall, still holding on to DeeDee for dear life as she caught her bearings.

They were both sweating and a little bit winded.

DeeDee pulled herself from inside of her and wiped her cum soaked hand on her own shirt. "I'll never wash this shirt again."

Bri looked up at her and wiped a sweat bead from across her lover's brow. "That's nasty."

ELEVEN

The line at Cameo was ridiculously long. They showed up a little before midnight hoping to meet DeeDee on the way in, but she was nowhere to be seen. Bri texted her for the third time.

We're outside. Still waiting.

"I don't know why she's not picking up."

Sunny reapplied lipstick using the phone as a mirror. "Maybe the hookup fell through. You know people always know people, but when it comes down to actually–"

"–No, she said she'd be here. She confirmed over two hours ago. She wouldn't stand me up...I hope."

"We should've gone in with those guys when they invited us," Kayla said.

"Of course you would," Bri said. "All of you have rings to hide behind. That one dude would be on my ass like I owe him something and I'm not up for the aggravation tonight. Just give me a few more minutes."

Charisse shuffled from foot to foot. "We have as long as my feet say we have in these shoes."

Bri tried calling DeeDee for the fifth time and got her voicemail again.

"Alright. Ten minutes. If she doesn't get back, we get in line like the rest of the peasants and get our own VIP."

"That works for me."

Bri was disappointed. In some way, this was a sign of true character. Someone who doesn't keep their word for the little things certainly doesn't keep their word for the big things. She couldn't stand a flake and after Q, she had little room for anyone who made promises they weren't willing to keep. They decided to wait in line and just a few minutes later, she saw DeeDee come out from the side door.

Her heart swelled and a strange sense of relief washed over her.

Bri stepped out of the line and DeeDee waved them over.

"My bad," she said. "I was running around in there talking to everybody and just checked my phone. Hope I didn't have you waiting too long."

Out of politeness, they said it was all good. Bri got another one of her hugs and DeeDee took a good look at all of them.

"Well damn. Is this how they make 'em in Chicago?"

"Well..."

They all took the compliment for themselves, patting their hair in place.

DeeDee led them through the dark and crowded space. Smoke filled the air while the base from the music blaring through speakers vibrated beneath their feet. Men ogled them with hungry eyes and women sized them up as they followed one another. Someone boldly grabbed onto Bri's hand which she pulled away from and kept moving. She remembered why she didn't go to clubs more often.

They passed the dance floor packed with men and women grinding on each other. They followed DeeDee up to the red rope the bouncer lifted without being prompted. VIP was a lot more tame, but it was no less crowded.

There were two other women sitting in the section DeeDee had reserved for them. She introduced them only as friends. Bri shot them a fake smile before taking a seat at the opposite end of the couch. She wanted to ask who they really were, but they were nowhere near that point in their relationship. They weren't even in a relationship.

DeeDee waved over one of the bottle girls wearing gold leotards and ordered a couple of things as the girls settled in.

The set up was a little awkward, not really knowing the two other women who were knee deep in their phones, shooting dirty glances at her from time to time, but the music was good and everyone mouthed the words of the song as they took in the space.

Not too far in the next section were a couple of guys surrounded by a group of women they probably hand-picked to grace them with their presence, yet their eyes were glued on them. One of them nodded in Bri's direction. He was fine, athletic build, tall, and looked like trouble, the kind of guy she would've allowed to talk to her while in college. But his breed was off limits for the moment. She was here with DeeDee and perfectly content with that.

She acknowledged him only with a tight smile and used her phone to busy herself.

"I ordered us some mixed drinks and a couple bottles so you can get whatever you want." DeeDee crouched down in front of her and placed a hand on her bare leg. Bri was a little self conscious about it, but it didn't stop the chills from coming.

"You look nice tonight," DeeDee said. "This dress is gonna make me fight somebody."

Bri shook her head. "Such a romantic."

The bottles came with a train of servers and a fireworks show. The alcohol flowed freely and everyone got friendly. The ladies even struck a conversation with the two women that seemed to warm up to them.

DeeDee disappeared and reappeared a couple of times. Every two minutes there was someone she had to greet or strike up a conversation with, as if she were making up for all that time she spent buried in her apartment.

Q was sort of like that, a social butterfly, someone everyone wanted to know and it brought her back to their time together. It wasn't all bad. In fact it wasn't bad at all. They worked as a couple and if it weren't for his inability to take things to the next level, she'd be living a different life in that very moment.

She hated that he still had such a hold of her heart, but it was only natural. He was slated to be the one she spent the rest of her life with. Those feelings don't just go away. It would take some time before she could fully get him out of her system. She hoped this thing with DeeDee would help the process along.

"Oou, this is my song," Sunny shouted over the music. They all got up, now a little saucy and danced in a group while rooting each other on.

As Bri half twerked to a song while sipping on her cranberry and vodka, someone decided to shoot their shot, grinding and rubbing on her ass with no shame. She whipped around to see who had lost their mind.

"Oh it's you," she said, as DeeDee rubbed on her booty. "I almost slapped the hell out of you."

"That's okay. I'd probably like it."

They nasty-danced in their own little corner as if there was no one there. Charisse was sure to say something about it later, but Bri no longer cared. She was lit from the inside out and she was dancing with the woman that had consumed her thoughts and dominated her time for the last couple of days.

She noticed immediately, the moment DeeDee seized up. She thought maybe something happened to her knees, but when she looked up, it was as if DeeDee had seen a ghost.

Bri followed her eyes to the VIP entrance where a woman stood waiting to be let in. She was beautiful, so the bouncer struggled with his decision to hold her off. She managed to talk her way in and DeeDee was no longer present.

"You okay?"

"Yeah, um. I'll be right back."

Bri joined the girls pretending to be unphased by DeeDee's sudden departure toward a woman that altered her mood on sight. She watched DeeDee from where she danced. This time, she wasn't flirting. There wasn't even a smile. In fact, it looked as though they were arguing.

She finally recognized the woman. Her hair was now short and she looked thinner, but it was her. Tori.

Charisse moved over to Bri as if she had something to tell her.

"That's Tori," she said. "Her ex from the show."

Bri didn't let on that she knew. It would make her look like she cared too much.

Tori's hands were in DeeDee's face now. It might've been her imagination, but Bri thought she pointed in her direction. They went back and forth for a bit, then Tori pushed her.

"Oh shit, I think they're fighting," Charisse said.

DeeDee put her hands up as if to say she wasn't going to return the favor, but the woman tried pushing her again only this time, DeeDee caught her hand and shuffled her off somewhere.

"Yep. They're definitely fighting."

Bri knew a lover's quarrel when she saw one. She had no claim on DeeDee so couldn't feel anyway about her exchange with her, but it did nothing to quell the uneasy feeling bubbling at the pit of her stomach. Still, she was determined to have a good time. She didn't want to be the one to spoil the evening because her crush scurried off with her ex somewhere. Even Kayla loosened up enough to give what she called a 'church' twerk on one of the guys which involved shaking her ass with no contact from him. 'Sorry boo. This ass is married.'

Sunny came over with a shot glass.

"Here chica. You look like you need this."

Bri threw back the shot and asked for another one. That one went straight to her bladder. She asked Sunny to come with her to the restroom.

The bottle girls pointed them to the nearest one and they locked arms as they made their way over. She didn't want to talk about what had gone down with DeeDee so she found something else to focus on.

"That guy you were talking to was cute," she said.

Sunny laughed. "Girl, today is his birthday. He just turned twenty-one."

"Oh damn. Go on, Cougar."

"Good to know after two kids, twenty pounds and carrying around a big baby of a husband, she's still got it."

They laughed and turned the corner when Bri stopped dead in her tracks. Sunny froze too and they stood there for too long.

Just a few hours ago, DeeDee had her coming up against a wall. She wasn't doing any of that with this Tori chick, but it felt far more intimate. DeeDee's hand was at her waist and Tori's head rested on her chest.

They looked up to find Bri and Sunny caught up like deer in headlights. It was either move forward or run off like they stole something.

Bri took the first step forward and Sunny followed behind. The awkwardness threatened to suffocate her as they passed the two and made it to the other side of the rest room.

There were two other women at the sink applying makeup, so whatever she wanted to say would have to wait.

She used the toilet with her ass in the air and was glad to see the women gone by the time she came out to wash her hands.

"What the fuck," she whispered. She washed the soap off her hand and grabbed too many napkins from it's holder. "I can't go back out there."

"Yeah you can. Do exactly what you did. Pretend they're not there."

She shook her head. "I can't. I can't do it. I'll wait fifteen minutes, then we'll go."

"Seriously?"

"I just can't. I'm fucking mortified."

Sunny watched her for a beat. "It's okay if you feel hurt."

"Why should I feel hurt? We met like a second ago."

"It's not about the quantity of time when it comes to these things. It's the quality and it's obvious whatever you two have going is intense and feelings are involved, even if it's been a second."

"I mean, I thought I had no expectations. I was just going with the flow. This was supposed to be fun."

"And that hasn't changed right?"

"So why do I wanna go tell that Tori bitch to back the fuck off of her?"

"Because you're possessive. You've always been. That's not new."

She couldn't argue with that. "That's probably why Q won't marry my ass. It's official. Imma die alone and childless with thirteen cats that eat my body before the police ever find me."

"Wow. You're being dramatic as hell right now. I'm sorry if things didn't work out as you hoped."

At this point, Bri couldn't tell if she was still mourning her relationship with Q or the death of the one she had already begun to fantasize with DeeDee. Perhaps the 'idea' of DeeDee was what she was truly falling for. How realistic was this going to be anyway, she rationalized. They barely knew each other, they lived miles away and more importantly, she wasn't even a lesbian. She could see now she had actually lost her mind.

It was all so clear now. DeeDee was just a distraction within a distraction and there was no excuse for letting herself get caught up like that. This is what happens when you step out of your comfort zone Bri.

"You're right," she said. "Fuck it. Let's go."

She grabbed her clutch and marched out of the bathroom, but DeeDee and her ex were gone. There was relief for a few seconds before she felt that overwhelming sense of disappointment.

"Come on," she said. "I'm about to get white boy wasted."

TWELVE

They slept through the morning. It was almost two when Bri dragged herself out of bed for something to drink. Her throat was dry and scratchy from puking up her guts just a few hours earlier.

"I feel horrendous," Sunny said, making her way to the kitchen for some gatorade they picked up knowing they'd have a day like this one.

"I look the way you feel," Bri said, taking a seat at one of the bar stools.

Charisse stepped out of her room with her eye mask still on her head. "I cannot believe I slept that long. I don't even remember how we got back here. I'm getting too old for this."

"Even Kayla got F'd up," Sunny said. "You know she can't hold her liquor."

Bri could barely muster up a chuckle.

Charisse came over and wrapped her arms around her. "You feeling better?" she asked with her chin on her shoulder.

Bri knew she was talking about DeeDee and not about the mess she made all over the half bath up front.

"Yes. I am. Thanks," she said, patting her arm to let her know she was in fact okay.

Truth was, she hadn't had much time to think about it. She woke up with the same anxious feeling she had before she blacked out. When she woke up, DeeDee was the first thing on her mind and she hated herself for it.

Not a single call. Even a simple courtesy text would've gone a long way. She didn't even have to explain herself, but at least she'd know, DeeDee saw her as more than some random hookup.

She wanted to drink the feeling away all over again, forget the whole week, get rid of this dreadful feeling that was sure to ruin the rest of the trip.

Without warning, she was getting another hug, by the both of them this time and it made her cry, uncontrollably, harder than she had ever cried in her life.

Once she was done, she wiped her face and picked up her phone.

"Who're you calling?" Charisse asked.

"Q. I think it's time."

Sunny grabbed the phone from her hand. "Oh no you don't."

"Excuse me. Can I get my phone back?"

"Friends don't let friends call their exes while hungover and in grief."

"What're you talking about? I thought you wanted me to get back with Q?"

"No, that's Kayla. I want you to do what's best for you. I like Q, but not if he's asking you to settle for less."

"I'm not going back to him. I just want to hear what he has to say."

"Don't do it," Sunny said.

"Give me the phone."

"I will...if you promise me you'll wait at least another twenty-four hours to call him."

Bri looked at Charisse. She'd be getting no help from her. She crossed her arms in defiance. "Fine. I promise. Can I have my phone now?"

Sunny didn't trust her, but she gave it back. Bri rubbed her temples. Defeated and exhausted, she headed back towards her room.

"Don't you call that man," Charisse shouted behind her.

She closed the door and leaned up against it. She didn't really want to call Q. She wanted to hear DeeDee's voice, wanted to be in her calming presence.

It was all probably for the best she decided. Maybe DeeDee was more like a crutch than a crush, something to lean on until her broken heart healed itself. All she needed was time.

She sat at the edge of the bed with her head pounding. Life would be so much easier if she could be one of those happy and single women. The idea had yet to settle on her. She liked being boo'd up, loved it really.

With her head hurting and her heart breaking, she put on headphones, put on her sad songs playlist, slipped in under the duvet and fell into another one of her deep bottomless sleeps.

◆◆◆

She woke up to a knock at the door. And then came another.

"Yes," she mumbled. The room was almost dark. She had slept through the afternoon too. The door creaked open and she winced against the light peering in from the living room.

Sunny stuck her head in. "We're going to hang out by the pool. You wanna come?"

Bri rolled over and turned on the lamp sitting on the nightstand.

"What time is it?"

"A little past seven."

"Alright. I'll meet you guys down there."

She washed her face and slipped into a bikini with a netted wrap. She hadn't eaten a thing all day. She made herself a sandwich while checking emails and made her way out.

As she entered the elevator, she fought the urge to push the number fifteen. No good would come from showing up to DeeDee's door uninvited, especially when she probably had a guest. Maybe she wasn't home at all, which was just as heartbreaking to think about.

Music was playing when she reached the poolside. It looked like a small party. There was a rollout bar with someone mixing drinks for the guests. Charisse and Sunny were dancing with two shirtless white guys who were probably on vacation themselves while Kayla was off under one of the lighted cabanas taking selfies.

A few people were splashing around in the water, but it was the two guys sitting at the very spot where she first met DeeDee that she focused on. Her chest tightened with the memory. One of them looked up to see her staring. He smiled with interest, and she smiled back, but that wasn't going to happen.

She decided to join Kayla. "Hey girl," she said, slipping onto the oversized outdoor bed next to her.

"They're giving out drinks over there."

"I'm good." Her phone buzzed and it made her heart skip a beat. To her disappointment, it was her legal assistant again.

Just wanted to let you know, Quinton passed by the office today. He left you a huge bouquet of flowers and a life sized teddy bear.

She sent a picture of the flowers with the bear sitting in the corner of the waiting area.

"Look at this mess," she said, showing Kayla the pic.

"That's sweet."

Bri gave her a side eye. She felt nothing. He had done this before. None of these gestures meant anything anymore.

You can either take them for yourself or give them away. Just get rid of them for me. Thank you so much.

"Can you take my picture for me?" She handed Kayla the phone. "Is the lighting good?" "It's perfect."

She took several shots for her to choose from. She chose the one where the water could be seen twinkling in the background.

Kayla put down her phone for a moment. "Uh oh."

"What?"

"Your girlfriend's here."

She looked up to find DeeDee giving some of the guys fist pounds at the makeshift bar. As usual, her body reacted wildly to the sight of her, and she steadied herself as her heart raced and her insides flipped on itself.

"She's not my girlfriend," she snipped. DeeDee had obviously come from somewhere and maybe she was with that Tori girl afterall.

Ex my ass. But dammit she was fine, dressed for a yacht party or an event somewhere near water, in a silk button down shirt, pink pants that rolled at the hem with all white Vans. Her hands were shoved in her pockets and she stood as if she were ready for a photo.

It was her goal to pretend DeeDee wasn't even there, only her eyes seemed to find themselves on her every few seconds. Did she even know she was there, Bri wondered. Was she simply passing by or did she intentionally make her way here. Based on her body language, she didn't seem to be searching for her at all.

Kayla did her best to keep things from getting awkward by making small talk, but Bri could hardly pay attention. She was too busy fake ignoring DeeDee who was now tapping on her knee. She was most likely talking about her injury and all things basketball which meant she'd probably be chatting it up forever.

"I think she's coming this way," Kayla said.

"Is she?"

Bri glanced up for a millisecond to see she had finally moved on from the bar and was gingerly making her way over to where Sunny and Charisse were. She must have just noticed them.

Both Sunny and Charisse pointed toward where she lounged with Kayla. DeeDee looked in her direction and her stomach clenched.

"Yep, she's coming this way."

"I can see that Kay. Thanks for the play by play."

"I'm gonna go call my man and leave you two to it."

"You don't have to."

Kayla scrunched up her nose and sauntered off toward DeeDee. They chatted for a minute. DeeDee laughed hard at something she said before moving on from each other. As DeeDee sauntered over her way, Bri allowed herself to make direct eye contact.

Her heart pumped in her throat. In just a couple of long strides, DeeDee was standing in front of her. She smelled like Spring.

"Do you mind if I sit here?"

"Not at all," Bri said casually. She moved her feet to give her space at the edge. DeeDee leaned forward and watched her the way she liked to do.

"Your girls are over there wildin'."

"Yep. Would you believe they're married?"

DeeDee tilted her head back and forth. "Married chicks can have a hot girl summer too.

"Except it's not summer."

"True."

DeeDee cleared her throat. She pulled her locs back off her face, but they only bounced back into place.

"You look nice," Bri said, in an attempt to diffuse the simmering tension.

DeeDee smiled. "Thank you. Had an investors meeting today," she said between quote fingers. My mentor flew into town and I caught up with him to go over the plans for the building. Told him what my lawyer advised," she said with a grin, "and he loved it."

Bri was relieved to hear it. She wasn't with Tori afterall, at least not all day, but she wasn't going to ask to confirm it. She relaxed her shoulders releasing the tension building there.

"He's even willing to cover some of the renovation costs to get things going."

"Wow. You've got the whole world wrapped around your little finger don't you?"

DeeDee laughed. "This smile is honey baby. Of course this means renegotiating some things, but things are moving."

Bri simply nodded as the music in the background filled the space between them.

"I was going to call you a little later, but I'm glad I found you here. I wanted to apologize for last night."

"Apologize for what?"

DeeDee almost laughed. She eyed her for a beat to see if she'd break character, but she didn't. "Well, I sort of bailed on you. My ex showed up and she kind of threw me off."

"Honestly, it's okay. We've been having a good time. You don't owe me an explanation."

"But I would like to."

"No need."

"So you're not upset?"

Bri made a face as if to say she had no idea where she would even get the notion. "Why would I be upset?"

DeeDee shrugged. "I'm sayin', you just seem a little passive aggressive right now."

Bri laughed dryly. "Passive aggressive? You haven't known me long enough to know when I'm being passive aggressive. Maybe you want me to be upset."

"I don't want that at all."

"Then, like I said, it's cool. Your girlfriend came through and you had to deal with her."

"My ex."

"Right. It doesn't matter either way."

DeeDee shook her head. "Don't do that."

"Don't do what?"

She reached for her leg, but Bri dodged her hold. It was a dead giveaway. She was upset and she was doing a bad job at hiding it.

DeeDee retreated. "I didn't expect her to be there, let alone be in town," she explained. "But I ran into her friends going into VIP and of course, they called her. The last we spoke, I told her I needed space to figure out my life. She told me that I could have all the space I needed because we were done."

"That's funny. She didn't look done with you."

"The truth is, she's engaged to a mutual friend."

Bri let the words sink in.

"Elaborate."

"After I broke things off with us the first time, she hooked up with a friend of ours. I was hurt when I heard about it, but they seemed happy. I gave my blessing just so things wouldn't be so awkward between us and the crew. Only I wasn't really over it, so I didn't make it easy for Tori to move on."

"Meaning?..."

DeeDee hesitated and averted her eyes. "Meaning, we were secretly still seeing each other up until my injury three months ago."

Bri took a moment to process her words. "So to be clear, you were backstabbing your friend who backstabbed you, by cheating with your ex?"

DeeDee nodded. "I did it mostly because I wanted to see them fail."

"Well look who's the petty one now."

"Never said I wasn't. I was in a bad place. And seeing them together wasn't good for me. Now they're getting married."

Bri rubbed her temples. "What in the name of reality t.v. is going on with you people?"

"I know. It's messy. Even for me. What you saw last night was the end of us. Took a while to get there, but I let her go. And I made sure she let go too. It was time."

Bri didn't know how to feel about this information. It sucked the magic and fun out of everything. This was a conversation for people working toward a serious relationship and that wasn't where they were.

It was complicated, but DeeDee was part of the complication. And if she was capable of something like this, what other lines was she willing to cross?

Unsure of what to say, she looked towards the people splashing in the water. Whether or not this would change things between them remained to be seen. It was all just too much for now.

"Look. This is a very confusing and emotional time for me. I hear you and I appreciate you telling me everything, but honestly, it's not that serious."

DeeDee placed a hand on her chest and clutched it as if she were wounded by her words. "Not that serious?"

"You know what I mean."

She leaned over and reached for Bri's leg again and this time, she let her latch on. Her hands were warm and felt soft against her skin.

"I've been miserable for a long time. I just did a good job hiding it. I was feeling lost about the trajectory of my career, my ex was fucking one of my oldest friends and I had no desire to try at life anymore." She paused for a beat as if struck with an epiphany. "Well I'll be damned. I guess I was depressed after all."

Bri stifled the chuckle that bubbled up unexpectedly. How this woman managed to make her laugh at a time like this was beyond her.

"I prayed for guidance on how to navigate this next phase of my life. Something told me to get out of my apartment and that night, you fall out of the sky like an angel. I'm telling you, what we have going on here, is divine in-"

Bri put a hand up. "Stop saying that. There's nothing divine about this and I sure as hell am no angel."

"Well you're *my* angel," DeeDee doubled down. "That's how I'll always feel about you regardless of what happens."

The dimples were on full display again, working their tricky little magic. Bri fought against their charm, but she was already losing.

She watched DeeDee tinker with her anklet. "It's crazy," she continued. "I feel like I've known you forever. You showed up right on time, gave me clarity, and the way I feel about you...I didn't even believe in soulmates until now."

Bri rolled her eyes. "You're laying it on thick don't you think?"

"Is it working?"

"Yes," she said. "And it's fucking scary."

"You don't think it's scary for me too?"

Bri hadn't considered it. For the most part, her confidence came off as fearlessness. If DeeDee was scared too, it meant she felt and understood the gravity of their connection. This wasn't just a vacation fling. There was more to this for her too.

DeeDee rubbed her thighs, eyed her hungrily. "I like this bathing suit. Out here lookin' like a whole shnack."

"You're a mess you know that?"

She moved in closer so they laid side by side now. She watched her as always and Bri crumbled under the intensity of her steady gaze.

"I like you...a lot," DeeDee said. "I'm in like with you."

Whatever wall she had built to guard her heart came crashing down with those words. Bri cracked a small smile.

"That's cute. I'm in like with you too."

DeeDee slid a hand across her bare waist, and Bri rested her arms around her neck. She pulled her in for a long and slow signature kind of kiss. It was the kind of kiss she'd never get used to.

"Get a room," someone yelled, breaking their bubble. It was Charisse making her life miserable again.

"Mind your business," Bri yelled back.

DeeDee pulled her back in with a tilt of the chin. "You leave in about two days right?"

"M-hm."

"I say we make the most of it."

"What'd you have in mind?"

DeeDee went quiet thinking about it. "Breakfast in bed? A long walk on the beach at sunset. Late night pillow talks sharing our deepest darkest secrets?"

"Wait. You have more secrets to share?"

"I was hoping maybe you did."

"Hm. I think I can dig up a few bones."

"Good. Right now though," DeeDee said, placing her lips on her ear, "there's only one thing I'd like you to do."

"Oh yeah? What's that?"

"Come upstairs and sit on my face."

Bri unfolded at the thought and brushed her lips against her lobe.

"Yes, please."

They barely looked at each other on the ride up to DeeDee's apartment. There was nothing but filth running through their minds. What was there to say about it?

As soon as DeeDee shut the door to her apartment, they were on each other like white on rice.

She helped Bri out of her bathing suit who nearly tripped in the process. Naked and already worked up, they kissed wildly as she helped DeeDee out of her shirt and shorts. Slowly, they inched themselves towards her bedroom. DeeDee reached down to pick her up by her thighs. She held on as DeeDee carried her the rest of the way.

"*Ouuu.* You *skrong*," Bri teased.

"I am. This is a whole lot of ass to carry," DeeDee said, tapping on its firm, plump surface. "I love this ass already."

She dropped her off on the bed with no warning and straddled herself over her. No further words spoken, just the kind of soul snatching eye contact Bri now required from a lover. Her heart hammered to a new rhythm.

Goosebumps.

No way these feelings stirring in her were real. No way were they to be taken as anything more than pure lust. But then, she reconsidered, lust had never felt like this.

DeeDee kissed her face softly, ran her lips along the indentation of her clavicle, kissed her breasts, sucked on her nipple, rinsed and repeated on the other as she ebbed a hand up, in between her thighs, all the way into her heated crotch.

Bri held on to her as DeeDee worked her down there, adding pressure to her pussy that had been slowly swelling with anticipation.

DeeDee watched her fall apart and she failed miserably at keeping it cute with her mouth hanging open like that. She panted, quieted her moans, rode the glide of her fingers, gritted her teeth at the building pleasure.

"You like that?" DeeDee asked, as if she didn't know how good it felt when she rubbed her thumb on her clit like that, round and round in circles. Her clit growing thicker under the stimulation, her pussy getting slicker by the second.

"M-hm. I like it a lot."

"You're so damn beautiful," DeeDee breathed into her ear, grinding into her slowly, disabling her limb to limb from the inside.

"Oh shit. That's it. That's so good," she heaved, feeling the pulse of her clit take over.

DeeDee pulled up from her and fell on to the bed on her back next to her. Before Bri could protest about the sudden move, DeeDee was welcoming her to climb aboard.

She did so willingly, moving up on her chest as DeeDee planted her hands on her ass. She moved her sauced up pussy over her face and found her mouth. Her clit effervesced under the heat of it as DeeDee sucked her in and squeezed her ass cheeks until they hurt so good.

Damn.

She held onto the headboard for balance, because she'd suffocate DeeDee if she didn't. She was having a hard time keeping her composure.

From there, she rolled her ass and spread her pussy all over her face, gave her a full cunt facial, whined while DeeDee dined as if she hadn't eaten in days.

As her eyes rolled up to the ceiling, her back arched and toes curled tight, her moans grew loud and indulgent. There was no way she'd be able to go back to any other kind of sex. Nor did she want to do it with anyone else. Maybe it was the oncoming orgasm doing all the thinking, the rise emanated deep down in her belly, but at this point, if this was wrong, this was the best mistake she had ever made in her life.

Fuck.

THIRTEEN

"I don't wanna go," Bri whined.

DeeDee held her tight and planted a lingering kiss on her forehead.

"What time is your flight tomorrow?"

"I don't know. Around one I think. She held onto DeeDee and squeezed. "I'm gonna miss you."

"What're you going to miss most about me?"

"The way you smell. I'd say your smile, but there's always Facetime. What are you going to miss about me?"

DeeDee was thoughtful for a quiet beat. "I'm going to miss being like this," she said. "I've never felt so comfortable around anyone so quickly."

Bri propped herself up on an elbow. "Really?"

"Really."

"That makes me feel really mushy inside."

"I'm also gonna miss this ass," DeeDee said, slapping it hard.

"Ouch," she wailed. It stung and grew hot where DeeDee made contact. She rested on DeeDee's chest and studied every inch of her pleasing features.

It was almost time to get back to the real world. Their time together felt like a dream and that was probably the thing she feared the most. Not that she had fallen for a woman, not that she had fallen so fast, but the fear that it was all just a fantasy that wouldn't hold up once she returned to normalcy.

When they weren't talking, sleeping or out eating, DeeDee was bringing her to climax, sometimes consecutively. She was spoiled and if for whatever reason it didn't work out, she would forever judge any sexual encounter by this experience.

Up to this point, she had been only a taker. Last night, she wanted to return the favor, make DeeDee moan her name for a change, make her buck, jerk and come at her command, but she put a pause on it again.

She didn't press the issue then, but time was running out and she didn't want to leave without knowing what she tasted like.

There was no time like the present. She moved from under the sheets and mounted her.

DeeDee's brows sat high on her forehead. "What are you doing?"

"You know damn well," she said, burying her face in her neck.

DeeDee laughed. "It's okay," she insisted. She pulled Bri away from the trail of kisses she was making south of her body.

"But I want to. Just tell me how you want it. I'm not only a fast learner, I'm a high achiever. A-plus student, teachers pet all day. I aim to please," she said, tracing a finger around her pert caramel colored nipples.

DeeDee ran her hands over her face. "Love that." She smiled for everything, but Bri could tell this was more nerves than anything.

"Wow. You're really turning red over this."

DeeDee scratched an eyebrow. She was deciding on how to explain what was obviously unresolved issues.

"It's not you. I promise."

"Explain then. No judgment. I just want to understand."

"I'm just really particular about how I want to be touched and the conditions have to be right."

"Okay, then let's make it right."

DeeDee shook her head. Bri wasn't getting it. She dismounted her if only to make her less squeamish.

"Believe me. I get all the pleasure I need from watching you get yours."

"Yes, and eventually, I would like to see you get yours as well. Healthy relationships require a balance of give and take."

"I get that. It's just a little more complicated for me, you understand?"

She didn't. She wanted to, but she had never met anyone who didn't want to be on the receiving end of pleasure. Of course she had only slept with men up until this point.

"Is this a lesbian thing?"

DeeDee's eyes disappeared behind a big cheeky smile. She shuffled herself up against the headboard and flipped her locs off her forehead. She let out a heavy sigh and let the smile drain from her face.

Bri gave her the space to speak and was willing to wait for as long as it took for her to dig deeper.

"When I was younger," she started, "I used to get touched...without my permission, from ten up until I was about thirteen years old."

Bri stared blankly. This was the last thing she expected to hear.

DeeDee composed herself. "She was a family friend who lived with us for a while. She used to babysit me when my grandmother was stuck in the hospital. Her boyfriend would come over and stay the night some times. They'd get high and sometimes when they got really high, they would have fun with me."

"Fun?" Bri repeated, unsure of its true meaning.

"Yep. That's what they'd call it. Fun."

Bri got it and now she felt sick to hear it. Even worse, now she was mortified by all of her cringey advances.

She was no psychologist, but she understood how that kind of trauma stuck to people, how it colored their world and dictated how they moved in it.

"I'm so sorry. If I knew-"

"-It's okay."

But it wasn't. She was angry on her behalf. "Who would do that to a child? Did you tell anyone? Are they still around?" Her questions flew out like darts and she regretted them right away. "I'm sorry. You don't have to answer that."

"I've never told anyone."

"Really? Not even your grandma?"

"Heck no. It would kill her to know that this woman she opened her house to did that to me. She'd never be able to live with herself. She just wants to see me happy, you know. Everything she's ever done was to make sure that I felt loved and happy."

"I don't even know what to say." She didn't know what to do either. She did only what felt right and wrapped her arms around her. She gave her a hundred kisses as if each one could replace all of her bad memories.

"I'm sorry that happened to you. But I appreciate you letting me in. If it's any consolation, I find you very well adjusted considering."

DeeDee chuckled. "Yeah, well, only I have this thing where I have to control everything surrounding being touched. It's a big production and we don't have the time."

"Well, how much time do we need?"

"More than you have. Don't you have to meet up with your girls?"

"Not really."

"It's your last day here, you probably should."

"Are you trying to get rid of me?"

DeeDee rubbed her eyes as she grew more squeamish by the second.

"Hey. I'm not trying to make you uncomfortable," Bri said, pulling her hands away from her face. "I just want to leave things in a really good place with us. We're going to be away from each other for a while."

"I'm good, babe. I promise."

Babe.

That stood out for her. Were they already at the pet name stage?

DeeDee rested an arm above her head and reached for her with the other hand.

"How about we save my turn for the next time we can be together like this?"

"Fine."

"I appreciate you wanting to," she said, pulling her in for a kiss. "It's the thought that counts."

"Well, Ms. Dorothy Divine. It would appear you are scared of something after all."

DeeDee winced as if it were physically painful to hear. Bri wasn't sure if it was for calling her by her full name or pointing out the chink in her armor.

"So no one's tried to reciprocate before?"

"Not really. I usually end up with a princess."

"Which is?..."

"Someone who only likes receiving." Bri shook her head. "Oh babe. You deserve so much more than that."

DeeDee reached out and wrapped a gentle hand around her neck. Bri held on to her wrist as they stared each other down. "And that's why I'm in like with you."

Bri grew misty. She chalked it up to hormones. It was close to that time of the month.

She rolled out of bed to get dressed. "So when do you think you can come up to see me?"

"I don't know honestly. I've got a whole lot of work to do with getting the building ready and I've gotta get things going with the clothing line."

"How about for my birthday? She slipped on one of DeeDee's oversized sweatshirts she planned on stealing. "It's in two months. I'll fly you up if you're too broke to do it by then, so no excuses."

"Ooh. So I got myself a shuga' mama? That's why you taste so sweet."

Bri let out a gut laugh. "I'm so done with you."

DeeDee's smile waned. The words hit differently now that she was close to leaving. "I hope the hell not," she whispered.

"Awww," Bri blushed.

She could already tell DeeDee was going to make leaving a little hard on the heart.

"Hey. You know we never did have that long walk on the beach. We've got a little time for that."

DeeDee was down. They made their way out and walked the path that led to the turquoise expanse of sea. The day was on the uncomfortable side of hot with an angry sun, no clouds in sight or wind to break the heat.

Bri pushed down her massive sun hat grateful for the shade it provided when they reached the destination.

They held hands and walked barefoot along the shore where the warm water met the edges of the sand.

"Tell me the truth," DeeDee started. "It won't hurt my feelings if you're just not feeling me like that. Okay, maybe it would a little."

"What is it?"

"Do you think you'd want to keep talking when you get back to Chicago?"

Bri couldn't help the rainbow of a smile that swept her face. DeeDee was essentially asking for some kind of long term communication. And of the serious kind.

"Talking? Like as friends? Or talking like... for more?"

DeeDee wavered. "Definitely for more. It's not everyday I meet someone I click with so easily. This feels different and I just want to hold on to this a little longer. I want to talk to you everyday."

Bri was a puddle of mush on the inside. She squeezed her arm and threaded herself around her.

"You're trying to keep me here aren't you?"

"Well can I?"

Bri couldn't find the joke in DeeDee's expression. She was serious and maybe that excited and scared her all at the same time.

"You're killing me. Let's keep talking. See where it goes."

"Okay," DeeDee said, squeezing her close. "That works for me. And I'm serious."

"I'm serious too."

"So you won't get weird if I call you three times a day?"

"No. Will you get weird if I want to stay on the phone for hours?"

"Never."

"You're so damn sure about everything."

"Not everything. But about this...about you...yeah. Definitely."

Bri looked up at her, feeling fully desired in a way she had always wanted. Here was this person she had only met yesterday ready to lock her down. It was either dangerous or courageous, but she was ready to jump in at the deep end knowing DeeDee had already proven, she wouldn't ever let her drown.

FOURTEEN

DeeDee offered to take them to the airport to see her off. They held hands in the car despite Bri's initial hesitation. Kissing was one thing, but those small moments of intimacy she found herself a little reluctant to show.

There wasn't much talking, singing or dancing. Everyone was exhausted from all that relaxation. The ride to the airport seemed so short despite that. Bri hated to see the sign that led to departures.

DeeDee pulled up to the curbside check-in and helped them place their luggages on the belt. It was time to say goodbye.

Sunny turned to her. "Thank you for the ride and it was nice meeting you, even though you stole our friend."

"Exactly," Kayla chimed in, poking her.

DeeDee held on to her arm. "Ouch."

"Oh I'm sorry."

She smiled. "I'm just playin'."

Kayla shook a closed fist as close to her face as she could reach. "Bri, your girlfriend's a fool."

She didn't fight the term girlfriend this time. "I know."

"Oh, I almost forgot," DeeDee said. She reached into the car and pulled out a photo from the dashboard. On it was an image of herself in uniform with a basketball under her arm. It was signed with a note that said, 'Leesha, Shoot for the stars...always. All the best, DeeDee.'

She handed it to Charisse. "You told me your niece was a fan."

Charisse took the photo. "A printed out headshot. Someone thinks highly of themselves."

"Well I am Instagram famous," DeeDee said smugly.

Charisse shook her head. "Thank you. I'm gonna get the favorite auntie prize with this one."

She made her way in with the others leaving Bri to say her final goodbye.

DeeDee stepped into her space and pulled her in close. Bri held on tight and didn't even mind all the eyes bearing witness to their same love. Her eyes began to gloss over and she felt silly about it.

"Call me when you get in."

"I will."

"This one's for the road," DeeDee said, reaching down to give her a small peck on the cheek. "And this one's 'cause I love you."

Bri didn't have a chance to react. DeeDee landed another long liquid kiss, and she willingly melted into it.

The world felt just a little on tilt as she walked to the gate with her friends. She waited in the airport for the plane to arrive with the words ringing in her ears. She still felt dizzy from it when she boarded the plane and was still free falling when the plane landed in O'Hara.

Chicago welcomed them home with a bit of late snow. They picked up their luggages and waited inside for their rides together. All the while, she held onto the little gift DeeDee had sent her off with. She would tell her friends eventually, but only after she had returned the sentiment. For now, she would keep it to herself. She didn't want them talking her into or out of anything.

Her ride came first. She gave each one of them big tight hugs.

"I'm one lucky chick to have you guys in my life. My day ones. My ride or dies. Love you guys. Even you Charisse."

Charisse gave her a heartfelt smile. "I love me too girl."

The ride home felt like a dream, nostalgic and unfamiliar all at once, as though something had changed. Maybe, she thought in retrospect, everything was exactly the same and she was the one who had changed.

She allowed herself to enjoy the high of being in love. How quickly it happened was of no consequence. Only time would tell just how deep the well runs.

The driver pulled up to the entrance of her building. He helped her remove the luggage from the car and she made her way in through the lobby.

Mr. Peters, the building resident's most liked security guard, was at his usual spot at the front desk on the verge of dozing off as usual.

"Hey Mr. Peters," she said.

"Oh man," he said, clutching his chest. "You scared me half way to death."

"So sorry."

"It's all right. Shouldn't been sleepin' no ways. But look at you, lookin' all rested and refreshed. Miami must have been good for you."

"Miami was exactly what the doctor ordered," she said.

"I'm glad to hear that. You got a couple of deliveries by the way. I'll have them sent up."

"Thank you, Mr. Peters. You have a good afternoon."

She took the elevator up and checked her emails on her phone. It was too much to glance through. She decided she'd look at them in the morning.

Tonight she was going to keep it light, spend her last few hours of freedom talking to her new favorite person.

She texted DeeDee:

I'm home. Talk to you when I get settled about that bomb you dropped. [mind blown emoji] [bomb emoji] [three heart eyes emojis]

She stepped into her apartment walking on air, so when she looked up from her phone she almost fell over.

"Quinton." Her heart pounded in her chest. "Wha-what are you doing here?"

He gave her a genial smile and got to his feet.

She almost didn't recognize him, wearing the full length wool coat she got him last year for his birthday. The full beard he was growing was now gone, giving way to the clean shaven, chiseled face she first met him with.

"How long have you been here?"

"Not too long. Kayla told me you guys had just landed. I still have the key and I'm still on the guest list. I let myself in so I could surprise you."

She scoffed. "Well you did that."

He pulled a Tiffany blue box out of his pocket she recognized and walked towards her in the way he did when he was feeling himself. In one smooth motion, he got on one knee, opened the box and looked up at her with longing.

"I've already asked you to marry me, so that's not what I'm here to do. I'm here to tell you that I've been a fool. I'm here to tell you that I can't see myself with anyone, but you. No more games. I'm ready to do what I should've done a long time ago." He took a deep breath. "Abrianna Rae Davis, will you take back this ring? I'm ready to be your husband, if you still want to be my wife."

She stared at him as if he were speaking a completely different language. She looked down at him, looked at the ring and then back at him.

His face brought back every feeling she had buried in the sands of Miami, all the emotions that had been diluted under the magic of DeeDee's embrace and it left her speechless.

"What do you say, baby?" he asked, with all the hope in the world in his eyes. "I think we should do it on July 17th."

He had her with that one. July 17th was her mother's birthday. He was playing dirty.

"I put a down on the venue you wanted. It's booked and ready to go just to show you how serious I am. This is it, baby."

This was more than he had ever done. She was inclined to believe him. She inhaled and exhaled with resignation feeling the overwhelm of too many emotions coming on all at once.

"This is all I ever wanted," she managed to get out.

He nodded. "I know, baby."

She composed herself and took in a deep breath.

Her phone buzzed. DeeDee had responded to her last text. She read the message.

I ain't scared. I said what I said. I love you. Te quero. Je t'aime. Missing you already. [sad face emoji] [broken heart emoji]

Her eyes slid back to him. The confusion in his eyes was apparent. She had read a text message while he was still on bended-knee, holding up a ring, still waiting for an answer.

"I'm sorry," she said flatly. "I'm gonna have to say no."

His face went blank for a moment. And then he seemed even more perplexed.

"I'm sorry. Did–did you say no?"

She shrunk into herself. "Yes. I did."

He shook his head as if he hadn't heard right, then stared at the floor as if she had dropped the right answer somewhere. He just needed to find it.

Slowly, he rose off his knee and stood before her. "I don't understand. I'm giving you the very thing you've been begging me for. I came here with my heart in my hand ready to commit and you say no? Why? What happened?"

Bri could see he was wounded. As much hurt he had put her through, she had no desire to inflict the same pain. She was in too good of a headspace, still walking on air. It was all good vibes. She simply didn't feel compelled to explain anything to him. He had his chance, and he blew it.

He slid his hands down his face, frustration etched in the lines of his forehead. He had finally come around to put himself completely out there and she was rejecting him without so much as a tear.

He looked at the ring in his hand and then gawked at her as though he expected her to change her mind at any moment.

He got nothing.

With a hard stare, he shoved the ring back in his pocket. "This is crazy."

"No, it's not," she said with all the confidence in the world. "It's just Divine intervention."

AFTERWORD

At the Deep End was my first dive into self publishing. I wrote it on a whim and since then I've been learning as I go along. This is an updated version of the original. The changes are subtle, but I think makes for a better reading experience. When I first wrote this story, I had no intentions of writing a sequel, but I'm a people pleaser, and I had several followers request a part two. I'm giving you four.

If you liked this book, I would love to know what you think about it. Please leave a review at your leisure. Feedback helps me craft more of the stories you want to read and keeps me motivated!"

While you're here check out lickherature.com for a Free Story: *When Nola Smiles.*

ABOUT THE AUTHOR

A creative soul, mother of three, wifey, and professional daydreamer, Deja was born and raised in a land of pristine beaches and palm trees called Miami. Her love for all things books started early. At eight, she wrote her first short story on a typewriter her mother gifted her so she'd stop writing on the walls.

Being able to share her stories has always been a dream and today, she writes steamy stories featuring queer and bi-curious women of color in various stages of love and relationships. Unfortunately, she doesn't guarantee happy endings, but dammit, you will be entertained!

When she's not dreaming up alternate universes, she's hanging out with her little tribe, watching something where the world ends or out restaurant hopping (now on Ubereats post Covid). Connect with Deja on the Gram @authordejaelise or visit www.lickherature.com for upcoming free stories and updates!

Made in the USA
Coppell, TX
14 December 2022

89175278R00104